SECRET MISS

STAR WARS®

THE CLONE WARS™

DUEL AT SHATTERED ROCK

BY RYDER WINDHAM
COVER ILLUSTRATED BY WAYNE LO

Grosset & Dunlap
An Imprint of Penguin Group (USA) Inc.

LucasBooks

GROSSET & DUNLAP
Published by the Penguin Group
Penguin Group (USA) Inc., 375 Hudson Street, New York, New York 10014, USA
Penguin Group (Canada), 90 Eglinton Avenue East, Suite 700,
Toronto, Ontario M4P 2Y3, Canada
(a division of Pearson Penguin Canada Inc.)
Penguin Books Ltd., 80 Strand, London WC2R 0RL, England
Penguin Group Ireland, 25 St. Stephen's Green, Dublin 2,
Ireland (a division of Penguin Books Ltd.)
Penguin Group (Australia), 250 Camberwell Road, Camberwell, Victoria 3124,
Australia (a division of Pearson Australia Group Pty. Ltd.)
Penguin Books India Pvt. Ltd., 11 Community Centre, Panchsheel Park,
New Delhi—110 017, India
Penguin Group (NZ), 67 Apollo Drive, Rosedale, North Shore 0632,
New Zealand (a division of Pearson New Zealand Ltd.)
Penguin Books (South Africa) (Pty.) Ltd., 24 Sturdee Avenue,
Rosebank, Johannesburg 2196, South Africa

Penguin Books Ltd., Registered Offices:
80 Strand, London WC2R 0RL, England

This book is published in partnership with LucasBooks, a division of Lucasfilm Ltd.

The publisher does not have any control over and does not assume any responsibility for author or third-party websites or their content.

ISBN 978-0-448-45566-2

10 9 8 7 6 5 4 3 2 1

CHAPTER 1

Cad Bane faced the two Gamorrean guards and said, "I'm here to see the Hutt."

The Gamorreans were stationed at their post, a wide, vaulted doorway that was the private entrance to their boss's headquarters on the largest asteroid in the Bilbringi system. They fixed their beady eyes on Bane and looked him over.

Bane, a blue-skinned Duros bounty hunter, had artificial breathing tubes embedded in his cheekbones and wore a broad-brimmed hat and long coat. The coat was pushed back to reveal twin blaster pistols holstered against his thighs, and he carried an old leather satchel in his right hand. Neither Gamorrean seemed impressed by the sight of the Duros or his weapons, but Bane noticed them shift their bulky forms slightly, getting ready to swing their heavy axes at him if he made a wrong move.

Slowly, carefully, Bane lowered the satchel to the stone floor, leaving it beside his right boot. Rising to his full height, he dipped his blue fingers into a coat pocket and removed two chips of precious metal. He placed one in each hand, then slowly extended his arms so the Gamorreans could see the chips that rested in his palms.

The nearest guard glanced at the offered chips while the other kept his own gaze fixed on Bane's holstered blasters. The nearest guard shifted his ax to his right hand, then snatched the two metal chips with his left. He lifted both chips up against the end of his broad snout. His nostrils flared as he sniffed at them. With a grunt of approval, he handed one chip to his partner, who took it greedily.

Bane smiled politely, waiting for the guards to step aside and let him pass through the doorway. Neither guard budged. The nearest guard held up his newly acquired metal chip and grunted what sounded like a question.

Bane's brow wrinkled upward. He said, "You want . . . more?"

The guard nodded.

Bane's red eyes flicked to the other guard, whose jowls twisted back into a stupid grin that revealed sharp, yellow teeth. "Very well." Bane sighed. "If it's more you want . . ." He tilted his head back, casually distracting the guards with the small motion of his hat's brim.

Neither guard saw the bounty hunter's hands flash to his holsters or the silencer-capped blasters leap into his waiting hands. Muffled pops sounded simultaneously from both barrels as Bane fired at the center of each guard's forehead. He rapidly returned his blasters to their holsters before he launched his hands forward and yanked the guards' axes from their suddenly slack fingers. The Gamorreans teetered, then collapsed dead upon the floor.

Bane dropped to a crouch and quietly placed the axes beside the guards' bodies. He pried their fingers back and quickly recovered the valuable metal chips that he had never meant for them to keep.

Pocketing the chips, he grabbed his leather satchel, then rose and stepped over the bodies, moving fast through the vaulted doorway to enter a dark corridor.

The official designation for the asteroid was Bilbringi VII. Its primary settlement was Bilbringi Depot. Although the Bilbringi system was located along a well-traveled hyperspace route, few traveled through the asteroid-choked system unless they had business with Drixo the Hutt, who owned the depot. Bane did in fact have business to discuss with Drixo, but believed it would be best if he arrived unannounced.

Bane held his satchel as he strode forward through the corridor. As he neared the corridor's end, his olfactory glands perceived a strange oily smell—the distinctive scent of roasted two-headed Effrikim worms.

The corridor emptied into a cavernous, shadowy chamber. A ring of yellow glow rods dangled from the black-rock ceiling and illuminated a wide, circular pit at the chamber's center. Smoke trailed up from the pit along with the sound of two high voices that were singing a lullaby in Huttese. The smell of roasted worms became more pungent.

Bane had expected to encounter more guards,

so he was not surprised as a dozen rushed at him from the shadows. Two guards were spear-wielding Klatooinians with olive skin and canine muzzles who jabbed at the sides of his coat. Behind Bane, an unseen guard pressed the tip of a blaster rifle's barrel up against the base of his skull. Bane had no doubt that the unseen guard was a Rodian. Only Rodians smelled that foul.

"I don't want trouble," Bane said, keeping his grip on the satchel while he raised his free hand. "I just need to see your boss."

The two singing voices stopped suddenly. A loud yawn rumbled from the pit, and then a deep, feminine voice bellowed, "An intruder? Let me see him before I have him skewered."

The Klatooinians removed Bane's blasters from their holsters and tucked the weapons into their own belts while the Rodian took the satchel. Bane slowly raised both hands in the air as the cluster of guards nudged him toward the edge of the pit.

Bane looked down and saw the singers he had heard. Two Theelin females, their pale skin mottled with crimson spots that matched their hair, snuggled against the curve of a massive Hutt's tail. The Hutt herself was a green-skinned sluglike creature with a pair of bulbous eyes and stubby-fingered arms. She was nestled beside a portable cooker, over which an assortment of two-headed worms sizzled on a slowly rotating spit.

The Hutt tilted her head back and gazed lazily at Bane. "Unless you have a remarkably good explanation for breaking into my private quarters and interrupting my snack time, I'll be eating Duros steaks for dinner."

Bane kept his hands raised. "I am a courier," he drawled. "Hired to bring one thousand peggats to Drixo the Hutt. The money is in the satchel that the Rodian took from me."

"Peggats?" Drixo's eyes glittered in the light of the glow rods. "Inspect the satchel!"

Bane heard a shuffling sound from behind, and then the Rodian moved up beside him at the edge of the pit. Facing Drixo, the Rodian said, "The bag's full of peggats, Your Hugeness."

Drixo looked at Bane. "I suppose that's how you got in here? By bribing my Gamorreans?"

Bane shrugged. "Good help is hard to find."

"Who hired you?" Drixo said suspiciously. "And

what exactly does your employer want from me?"

"My client wishes to remain anonymous." Extending his fingers to gesture at the walls and ceiling, Bane said, "He wants to purchase Bilbringi Depot."

Drixo laughed. "My property is worth more than one thousand peggats. Much more."

"My client is very determined . . . and very generous. If you name your price, I am sure he will—"

"Your client means nothing to me. My asteroid is not for sale."

"I see," Bane said. "In that case, I shall take my satchel and leave you in peace."

Drixo sighed. "You may leave, but with an empty satchel. The peggats stay with me."

"Hmm." Bane grimaced. "I don't think my employer will like that very much."

"He doesn't really have a choice. Nor do you." Drixo bit off both heads of a roasted worm. "Consider yourself lucky that I don't order my men to flay you alive from here to the Comra system, and then do something really awful to you."

Drixo's guards had a good laugh at this. Bane glanced at the two Theelin and saw they were laughing, too. He wondered if the Theelin laughed out of fear or loyalty to their Hutt master. Returning his gaze to Drixo, he said, "Perhaps there is another possibility. Perhaps I might . . ."

"Yes?" Drixo said impatiently. "You might what?"

"Kill everyone in the room."

A roar of blaster fire exploded from the entrance of the corridor behind Bane. Having followed the Duros's path, three IG-86 sentinel droids with cylindrical, drumlike heads and lean, gray-metal bodies lurched into the chamber with their weapons blazing, spraying energy bolts at every life-form above Drixo's pit except for Cad Bane.

Bane stepped back from the edge of the pit and watched his sentinel droids mow down the guards. The Rodian squeezed off a single shot of return fire before a droid cut him in half. The two Klatooinians were so distracted by the sneak attack that they did not notice Bane reach to their belts to retrieve his blaster pistols. Bane fired two precise shots at point-blank range. Both Klatooinians dropped their spears and crumpled to the floor.

The sentinel droids stopped firing. Bane's red

eyes swept over the chamber to confirm all the guards were dead before he returned to the edge of the pit. He aimed one blaster at Drixo's head and the other in the general direction of the two Theelin.

Seeing Bane's blaster, both Theelin hissed loudly as they reached for their own concealed weapons, a matching pair of curved-blade throwing knives. One Theelin managed to fling her knife up at Bane, and the other was about to do the same, but Bane—realizing the Theelin were loyal to Drixo—ducked fast and let his blaster spit twice. The thrown knife whizzed past Bane's head at the same moment that both Theelin dropped and flopped against the Hutt's tail.

Drixo looked at the bodies slumped beside her. Lifting her gaze to meet Bane's, she said, "You didn't have to kill my pets."

"And they didn't have to throw knives at me," Bane answered dryly as the three sentinel droids moved up beside him. "All your guards are dead, Drixo. Most unfortunate. If only you had not insisted on keeping Bilbringi Depot." He gave a slight nod to the three droids. The droids aimed their own blasters at the Hutt in the bottom of the pit.

"Wait!" Drixo said. "I . . . I will gladly sell Bilbringi Depot to you!"

"Sell?" Bane shook his head. "Sorry, Drixo. I should have told you. The peggats were a one-time-only offer. My client was most insistent about that."

"Did I say *sell*?" Drixo said. "Sorry, I meant to say I will gladly *give* Bilbringi Depot—and the entire asteroid—to you."

"Really?"

"Yes! You can take everything!"

"But I already have," Bane said. "Fire at will."

The droids obeyed as usual.

"Bilbringi Depot is secured," Cad Bane reported.

"You have done well, bounty hunter," said the Sith Lord Darth Sidious. With his hooded head facing the hologram projector, he was seated in his secret lair in an industrial district of skyscrapers on Coruscant. As the flickering three-dimensional image of Bane returned to his gaze, he continued, "I trust you left no evidence of your work."

"I never leave a mess unless I'm paid to leave a

mess," Bane replied curtly. "I'm a professional."

"Payment has been transferred to your account. I shall contact you when I next require your services." Darth Sidious broke the connection, and Bane's hologram vanished. He pressed a button on the communications console, and a different hologram appeared before him.

The hologram represented Count Dooku, a former Jedi Master who had become the leader of the Separatists and the Confederacy of Independent Systems. An older man with a piercing gaze and immaculately groomed beard and mustache, Dooku was secretly Darth Sidious's Sith apprentice, Darth Tyranus. Dooku's hologram bowed, then said, "What is thy bidding, my Master?"

"We have Bilbringi Depot. Is the Techno Union ready to transport ship-building materials?"

"Yes, my Master. I shall contact Overseer Umbrag and instruct him to deliver the materials to Bilbringi immediately."

"And what of your captive Jedi?"

"Ring-Sol Ambase is still recovering. But he will soon be ready to carry out the next step of our venture."

"Excellent."

"All is proceeding as you have foreseen," Dooku said with admiration. "Republic forces have liberated the planet Kynachi and established tentative diplomatic relations with Chiss space. Bilbringi Depot is ours, and the once neutral Kynachi intends to ally with the Republic."

"And as we speak," Darth Sidious added, "Langu Sommilor, a representative from Kynachi, is bound for Coruscant. His ship is scheduled to refuel on the planet Vaced. And not by coincidence, the freighter that carries Nuru Kungurama and Breakout Squad is traveling the same hyperspace route. It would be advantageous to have Kungurama and Sommilor meet on Vaced."

Dooku smiled. "Our plans for Bilbringi can be accelerated."

"Kungurama's visit to Vaced should be . . . unfortunate."

"Master, this is a perfect opportunity to enlist our associates on Mandalore."

"Yes," Darth Sidious hissed. "Yes. Contact the Death Watch. Tell them you require their best sniper."

CHAPTER 2

Holding a battle club high over his broad head, the stony-muscled monster with a face in the middle of his torso dodged the long-limbed desert-predator's spear as he jumped over a small four-legged creature's spiked tail to land beside a giant savage with leathery skin and a snakelike head. The snake-head savage turned fast and seized the monster's club. The furious monster tried to grab its club back but stumbled into the waiting claws of a vicious beast with a lashing tail.

Then the hulking savage did the unthinkable and swung the stolen club at his own ally, a hook-nosed insectoid. The powerful swing sent the insectoid flying into the clawed beast, which shrieked before it vanished, along with the insectoid and the stony-muscled monster, from the hologame table. "That's against the rules!" said the clone trooper Knuckles as he slammed his bare fist onto the edge of the game table, making the smaller holographic monsters jump. "You're not supposed to steal weapons and sacrifice your own holomonsters to win like . . . like that!"

"I made a fair move," replied the reprogrammed droid commando named Cleaver. "Screaming about it won't help you."

"But you can't!"

"Sir, I admit I possess only rudimentary knowledge of the game dejarik," Cleaver said patiently, "but I believe the combination of the tri-sector sidestep and the carnivore volley is entirely acceptable according to the rules in the Corellian edition of *Dejarik for Amateurs and Children*."

Knuckles and Cleaver were seated on opposite sides of the hologame table in the main hold of the *Hasty Harpy*, a Corellian YT-1760 transport that was presently traveling through hyperspace along the Namadii Corridor, on course for the planet Coruscant. On the other side of the hold, the *Harpy*'s captain, Lalo Gunn, sat beside the clone trooper

Chatterbox. Gunn was teaching Chatterbox how to play sabacc, a card game. Hearing Cleaver's remarks, Gunn chuckled and said, "Tough luck, Knuckles. You just got beaten by a droid."

Knuckles tapped the hologame table with his index finger. "Care for a rematch, Cleaver?"

"If it would please you, sir."

"Hang on, you two," interrupted another clone, Breaker, who was hunkered in front of a nearby engineering console's lower access cabinet. "Don't start the next game until Sharp and I finish this systems check." He glanced up at Sharp, who stood beside him. "Press the three switches now."

"Okay," said Sharp. He pressed the switches and held them in place. Like Knuckles, Chatterbox, and Breaker, Sharp was not wearing his helmet at the moment. All four men were identical and resembled Jango Fett, the notorious bounty hunter who had served as the genetic template for the Kaminoan-produced clone soldiers of the Republic Army.

Breaker looked away from the console's cabinet to face the *Harpy*'s one remaining passenger, a boy with red eyes, blue skin, and black hair. Breaker said, "We should be done in a moment, Commander."

The young Jedi Nuru Kungurama, a Chiss who had been raised in the Jedi Temple on Coruscant, responded with a nod. Seated with his back against a padded bulkhead, Nuru maintained a passive expression as he watched the others. But his mind was hardly relaxed.

Nuru had never imagined he would find himself in command of a squad of Republic clone troopers fighting Separatist forces on distant worlds. But ever since he had left the Temple to follow his Master, Ring-Sol Ambase, on a secret mission to the planet Kynachi, his life had taken many unexpected turns.

Becoming separated from his Master in orbit of Kynachi. Meeting the former smuggler Lalo Gunn just before they encountered a mysterious Duros bounty hunter. Learning that the Techno Union had conquered Kynachi and secretly occupied the world for a decade. The destruction of Gunn's navigation droid, Teejay, whose brain was utilized for the construction of Cleaver. The formation of Breakout Squad. Fighting the Separatist Overseer Umbrag and his Techno Union droids. The liberation of Kynachi. The recovery of Ambase's lightsaber.

What happened to my Master?

And then the mission to distant Chiss space, and Nuru's first encounter with another Chiss. The sneak attack by Overseer Umbrag. The bizarre encounter with the Black Hole Pirates . . .

How did we wind up near that uncharted black hole?

Sharp had confided that he suspected their unexpected detour to the black hole sector had not been an accident—that an unknown enemy might be manipulating their movements across the galaxy. Even more troubling, Sharp surmised that the *Harpy's* navi-computer had been rigged to alter the ship's course. And if Sharp was right . . .

We may have a traitor on board.

Because clone troopers were engineered to serve and obey their Jedi leaders, Nuru had a hard time with the idea that any of the clones could be traitors. As for Lalo Gunn, he could not imagine any reason why she would have deliberately flown her ship to that wretched black hole sector.

Are we really being manipulated? Is someone playing a dangerous game using us as pawns?

A fresh set of holomonsters appeared on the table before Knuckles and Cleaver. Knuckles said, "Hey,

Breaker. When you refurbished Cleaver's brain, you didn't program him to be a dejarik grandmaster, did you?"

Breaker shook his head. "No, but Cleaver's a fast learner."

"Just my luck," Knuckles muttered as one of Cleaver's holomonsters began clobbering another.

Nuru was struck by a sudden thought. *If Breaker is a traitor, could he have reprogrammed Cleaver to tamper with the navi-computer? What if—?*

Nuru's musings were interrupted by a loud beep. All eyes turned to the main hold's comm.

"That's the hypercomm signal," Gunn said. She tossed down her cards and went to the comm. "Someone's hailing us." She looked at Breaker and Sharp. "I switched off the hyperspace transponder so no one could track us. Did either of you clowns activate it?"

"No," Breaker said as he stepped beside Gunn. Pointing to the comm's data display, he looked to Nuru and said, "Commander, we're receiving an emergency transmission from Coruscant."

Nuru leaned forward on his seat and said, "Open it."

Gunn pressed a button on the console. Two low-resolution holograms materialized in the air above the comm. Everyone in the *Harpy*'s hold recognized the flickering images as Jedi General Yoda and Supreme Chancellor Palpatine.

"Uh, Captain Gunn here," Gunn said sheepishly, not sure how she should address either the Jedi Master or the elected leader of the Galactic Republic.

As Nuru rose to his feet, he felt a clinking sound at his hip. He kept forgetting that he now had two lightsabers—his Master's as well as his own—clipped to his belt. Bowing slightly at the holograms, he said, "Master Yoda. Chancellor Palpatine."

"Ah, Nuru Kungurama," Palpatine's voice crackled. "Thank goodness my pilots were able to locate Captain Gunn's ship. We knew it was likely you'd return to Coruscant by the Namadii Corridor."

Nuru suspected he was about to be questioned about the mission to Chiss space. He said, "I regret my meeting with the Chiss ambassador was not very successful, Chancellor. We—"

"That discussion will have to wait," Palpatine interrupted.

"A new concern, we have," Yoda added.

Palpatine gestured to his left, and a hologram of another man materialized. Palpatine said, "Allow me to introduce Commissioner Langu Sommilor, a representative of Kynachi."

Sommilor appeared as a lean man with thinning gold hair. "Greetings, Nuru Kungurama. I'm sorry you left Kynachi before I could personally thank you for bringing an end to the Techno Union's ten-year occupation of my world."

"You give me too much credit, Commissioner. Without my companions, I could not have . . ." Nuru's words caught in his throat. Forgetting all protocol, he said, "Master Yoda, has Master Ambase been found?"

Yoda's hologram appeared to shudder slightly. "Still lost, Ambase is."

Sommilor added, "I have many volunteers looking for Ambase on Kynachi, but so far we have found no sign of him."

Palpatine said, "Young Kungurama, be assured we are making every effort to locate your Master. He will be found."

Nuru frowned. He was unable to hide his disappointment.

"The reason for this communication," Palpatine continued, "is to inform you that Commissioner Sommilor is also traveling the Namadii Corridor. Kynachi intends to ally with the Republic, and the commissioner is coming to Coruscant for a special meeting with the Senate. Unfortunately, Republic Intelligence has reason to believe the Techno Union will attempt to stop the commissioner from reaching his destination. The Jedi Council informed me that no Jedi were readily available to escort the commissioner, but then I thought we might manage to contact you before you returned to Coruscant."

Turning to Yoda's hologram, Palpatine added brightly, "It's remarkable how things worked out, isn't it?"

"Hurmm," Yoda muttered without enthusiasm.

Sommilor said, "I'm traveling in a Suwantek Systems freighter that will be refueling on the planet Vaced in approximately six standard hours. Can you and your squad meet me there, and then escort me to Coruscant?"

Nuru looked at Gunn. Gunn said, "Last I checked the navi-computer, Vaced was still ahead of us, less than five hours away. We could get there before the commissioner."

Returning his attention to Sommilor's hologram, Nuru said, "I am at your service, Commissioner."

"Thank you again, Nuru Kungurama. I look forward to meeting you on Vaced."

Palpatine smiled. "And I look forward to meeting you *all* upon your arrival at Coruscant. And, Nuru, I greatly anticipate your full report about the Chiss ambassador."

Yoda nodded to Nuru. "May the Force be with you and your allies." The holograms flickered off.

Rising from the hologame table, Knuckles stretched his arms. "Well, so much for our recreation hour." He shut down the game. "Better luck next time, Cleaver."

"But I was winning again," Cleaver said as the holomonsters vanished.

Knuckles looked at the comm console. "Good timing on the chancellor's part, wasn't it?"

Nuru said, "What do you mean?"

"If the chancellor and General Yoda had contacted us later, we might have already passed Vaced. We would have had to exit hyperspace at some other point on the Namadii Corridor and then double back to Vaced to meet the commissioner."

Chatterbox cleared his throat, then said, "I have a bad feeling about this."

Everyone looked at Chatterbox. Gunn said, "What are you jabbering about?"

The usually silent trooper cleared his throat again. "General Ambase was lost on Kynachi. We're traveling through hyperspace with you, Ambase's apprentice. A ship from Kynachi is trailing us on the same hyperlane. Both ships are bound for Coruscant." Chatterbox shook his head. "Too many coincidences."

Gunn scowled. "That's the most words I've heard out of you. Ever."

Ignoring Gunn, Nuru said, "You think we're being set up?"

Chatterbox nodded.

"But who's pulling the strings?" Knuckles said with a broad shrug. "If it's Overseer Umbrag and his Techno Union cronies, they've been doing a sloppy job. We defeated them at Kynachi *and* helped chase them out of Chiss space. So who else could be messing with us?"

Breaker was watching a scope on the comm

board as he responded, "Probably whoever planted a tracking device on the *Harpy*."

"Huh?" Gunn said. "What tracking device?"

"Look here," Breaker said, gesturing to the scope. Nuru and Gunn moved closer to view the data display for the *Harpy's* communications systems. "Watch for the blip."

Gunn said, "I don't see any—"

"Wait," Breaker said. A moment later, a tiny green circle flashed on the data display. "That's the third blip in the past minute. It's an intermittent broadcast signal. I can't pinpoint the source, but it's definitely coming from somewhere on the *Harpy*."

"Well, I'll be fried," Gunn muttered.

Knuckles tapped the side of his head. Looking at Nuru, he said, "The Black Hole Pirates. Maybe they slapped the tracker on us."

"Here's another possibility," Breaker said. "Maybe the Techno Union planted tracking devices on every grounded starship during the occupation of Kynachi. If that happened, they could be tracking Commissioner Sommilor as well as us."

"Also by tuning into our transmissions," added Gunn. "Blast! That could explain how Umbrag wound up following us straight to Chiss space."

Nuru said, "According to the chancellor, Republic Intelligence believes the Techno Union will try to stop Sommilor, but . . ." Nuru shook his head. "I'm not convinced the Techno Union is responsible for the transmitter. Like Knuckles pointed out, if they're trying to manipulate us, they don't seem to be doing a good job."

Knuckles said, "Should we send a warning to the commissioner?"

"No," Nuru replied. "Not unless we can determine that it's safe. Tracking devices might not have been the only thing planted. For all we know, sending a warning transmission could trigger a concealed explosive."

Breaker asked, "How do you want to proceed, Commander?"

"We're going to carry out our orders and see this mission through. And we're going to be very, very careful. Breaker, you'll reset the navi-computer to exit hyperspace at Vaced. The rest of us will search the ship's interior for the tracking device."

"But what if the transmitter isn't inside the *Harpy*?" Gunn asked. "What if it's on the hull?"

"Then we'll search the hull after we land on Vaced."

Breaker exited the hold and went to reset the navi-computer. Nuru said, "Sharp and Chatterbox, you search the starboard hold and maintenance bays. Knuckles and Cleaver, you cover the port side. I'll look here, and Gunn will look aft."

"Excuse me, Commander," Cleaver said. "What does a tracking device look like?"

"It could be a small box or compact case, probably with a magnetic back so it can be easily attached to a bulkhead or other surface. It might be camouflaged."

Cleaver looked up at the maintenance access hatch on the ceiling and said, "I have found something."

"Really?" Nuru asked. "What is it?"

Cleaver reached up and grasped a metal box that was magnetically secured to the hatch's frame. Pulling the box away from the frame, he said, "Is this the transmitter?"

Gunn laughed. "No, Cleaver. That's a tool kit. See?" Taking the box from the droid, she slid back the box's lid to show him the tools inside.

"Oh," Cleaver said. Gunn sealed the tool kit and placed it back up against the frame.

"Come on, Cleaver," Knuckles said. He headed out of the main hold with the droid at his heels.

Chatterbox, Sharp, and Gunn exited the hold, leaving Nuru behind. As Nuru began searching every nook of the nearest bulkhead for a hidden transmitter, more thoughts raced through his head. *Maybe there isn't a traitor on board. Maybe some devious enemy was somehow responsible for sending us to the black hole sector. Maybe . . .*

Maybe I have absolutely no idea who I can trust anymore.

Nuru sighed. He wished he could ask someone for guidance. He touched the second lightsaber at his belt.

What would Master Ambase do if he were here right now?

And then Nuru swallowed hard. Ever since leaving Kynachi, he had held firmly to his belief that Ring-Sol Ambase was still alive. But now, as the *Hasty Harpy* carried him toward an increasingly uncertain future, he wondered if Ambase might really be gone forever.

CHAPTER 3

"Ring-Sol?" said Count Dooku. "Can you hear me?"

The Jedi Master Ring-Sol Ambase was lying on an elevated pad in the makeshift medical chamber, an eight-walled room with a single window. He opened his eyes to see Count Dooku, the former Jedi and current leader of the Separatists, standing at his bedside.

A dark-haired clone trooper wearing a gray tunic with matching pants and black slip-on shoes stood against one wall. Two super battle droids were positioned on either side of the clone, their blasters aimed at his torso.

Dooku smiled at Ambase and said, "Good morning, old friend."

Ambase's eyes shifted to the window, which offered a view of the same gray sky he had seen earlier, the last time he was conscious. "Morning?" he muttered, and immediately realized that a breath mask no longer covered the lower half of his face. "Where?"

"Still at my retreat in the Bogden system," Dooku said. "You've been here for over a week."

Memories crashed like waves through Ambase's mind. The destruction of his freighter in orbit of the planet Kynachi. Blacking out in a gas-filled escape pod that also carried five clone troopers. Awakening in the eight-walled room with Dooku. The clone trooper who claimed he and Ambase had become separated on Kynachi, and also that he had no memory of finding Ambase or leaving Kynachi. The holorecording that appeared to confirm Ambase's Padawan apprentice, Nuru Kungurama, had been a stowaway on the doomed freighter.

Ambase cleared his throat. "Dooku . . . what do you want?"

"You are not my prisoner, Ring-Sol. I only

brought you here because you needed help desperately." He gestured to the medical regulators and diagnostic machines on the other side of the bed. "All readings indicate your pulmonary system has improved."

"You kept me . . . alive?"

"Perhaps you don't remember, but I did promise your safe return to the Jedi Temple. However, you are hardly fit to travel. I believe it would be best if you remained here for a few more days."

Ambase had no reason to believe Dooku was telling the truth. He kept his expression neutral.

Dooku patted Ambase's shoulder. "When you are strong enough, a nonmilitary transport will be waiting to deliver you to Coruscant. But, Ring-Sol . . . I hope you understand that no one is safe in the Republic. You remember what I told you about Darth Sidious?"

"Yes," Ambase rasped. "I . . . remember." In fact, Dooku's assertion that a Sith Lord named Darth Sidious was controlling members of the Senate had not been news to Ambase. Like other Jedi Masters, he had reviewed Obi-Wan Kenobi's report about Dooku and the Battle of Geonosis. And like

Obi-Wan, Ambase could only guess whether Dooku was lying.

"And you also recall the holorecording?" Dooku continued. "The one this trooper recovered from the freighter that was destroyed at Kynachi?" Dooku gave a slight nod toward the captive clone.

Ambase glanced at the clone. "You told me your name is . . . Sharp?"

The clone responded with a nod.

Dooku said, "While the recording presented no proof that your apprentice sabotaged the freighter before it reached Kynachi, it is my understanding that you were unaware he had concealed himself in a utility closet near the engineering station. Evidently, he not only survived the ship's destruction, but assumed command of your troops."

Ambase wondered whether the clone had talked too much to Dooku. He shot a glance at the clone. The clone grimaced.

Dooku shook his head sadly. "I cannot imagine any good explanation for Nuru Kungurama's actions and I admit I fear the worst. The Sith Lords *are* manipulating the Jedi Order as well as the Senate. We have to allow the possibility that the Sith have turned Jedi apprentices against their own Masters."

Nuru? In league with the Sith? Despite Ambase's Jedi training to suppress emotions, he felt a rush of outrage at Dooku for suggesting the possibility.

Dooku placed his hand gently on Ambase's shoulder. "By the Force, I hope Nuru is innocent of any wrongdoing. For if he is not . . ." Dooku withdrew his hand. "Make no mistake of my goals in this war, Ring-Sol. The Sith must be destroyed."

Hearing this, Ambase felt something even more unexpected. A small stab of fear.

"It recently came to my attention," Dooku continued, "that Nuru has seized Bilbringi Depot. It may be just a rumor, but . . ." Distracted, he looked to the room's only doorway and saw a small droid with an antennae extending from the top of its head waddling into the room. The droid came to a stop before Dooku.

"Excuse me, Master," the droid said. "Your presence is required on Landing Pad three." The small droid then turned around and waddled out.

Dooku backed away from Ambase's bed. "I have to attend to a tiny matter, and then I shall also prepare a transport so you may depart when you wish." He signaled the super battle droids, who stepped away from the clone and filed quickly out of the room. As the droids clanked away, Dooku faced the clone and added, "You may remain with your commander, but the droids will be just outside." And then Dooku strode off, his cape flowing like a dark wave behind him.

The clone watched the doorway and listened for a moment, then raised one hand to casually pinch his earlobe. Ambase had no difficulty comprehending the clone's gesture. *The Separatists are probably listening.*

Ambase studied the clone's swarthy features. The clone was identical to the others in the Republic's army. Despite the clone's appearance, Ambase silently questioned his identity and origin.

Can clones be brainwashed? Can they lie? Or is this man even a clone? Could he be a surgically altered Separatist impostor? The Jedi could not think of any way to prove the man had been a member of the ill-fated task force sent to Kynachi, let alone that he was the trooper named Sharp.

Ambase looked to the window. "We're in the Bogden system?"

"I can't say for certain, sir," the clone replied. He moved to the window and rapped his knuckles against it. "Feels strong, like transparisteel." Transparisteel was a completely transparent metal alloy commonly used for starship viewports as well as windows for buildings that required heavy security.

"What's outside?"

"Landing pads. Three ships. It's raining hard. I think one ship is Dooku's solar sailer. Another looks like the Kuat transport that we were in when the battle droids found us. It appears some astromech droids are repairing it now."

"What about the third ship?"

"I don't have a clear view of it, sir. Too much rain."

Ambase flexed the fingers of his right hand. "I don't suppose you've seen my lightsaber? Or my utility belt?"

"No, sir. Like I told you earlier . . . One moment I was searching for you on Kynachi. The next thing I know, I'm waking up behind the controls of a crashed transport with a bump on the back of my head. I found you unconscious, strapped into a bunk in the hold. Then the droid commandoes arrived."

The clone rubbed the back of his head. "If the droids took your lightsaber, I didn't see them do it."

"How did we get from the crashed transport to this place? Spacecraft?"

"No, sir. The droids brought us here directly in an airspeeder."

Still looking out the window, Ambase said, "Of all the worlds in the galaxy, we somehow wound up on one where Count Dooku has a hideout."

The clone rubbed the back of his head again. "If only I could remember what happened on Kynachi."

Ambase looked at the clone. "I hope you haven't been . . . mistreated."

"No, sir. The droids have me in a nearby cell. They tried questioning me, but I didn't talk."

"But Dooku learned Nuru was at Kynachi."

The clone grimaced again. "I didn't tell him, sir. The Separatists got our freighter's log when they captured me. When Dooku viewed the log's holorecordings, he recognized Kungurama immediately."

Ambase smiled. "I would have been more surprised if Dooku had not recognized Nuru, and not just because Nuru is so distinctive." Ambase returned his gaze to the window. "Eleven years ago, when I found the boy in an escape pod at the edge of Wild Space . . . Dooku was with me."

"Dooku was still a Jedi then?"

"That's right."

The clone was about to ask another question when a clanking sound indicated the droids were about to reenter the chamber. Speaking in a rushed whisper, Ambase said, "You have to get us out of here."

"I'm working on it, sir," the clone replied, just as the droids walked in.

A heavy rain was falling as Count Dooku stepped out of his castle, a spired structure perched atop a mountain on the Bogden moon Kohlma. In one hand, Dooku carried Ambase's utility belt. As he proceeded to the starship landing pads, a disc-shaped repulsorlift device traveled through the air above his head, projecting a thin energy shield to deflect the rain from his body.

Dooku walked past his own solar sailer, which

rested on Landing Pad one, and also past the next pad, where a team of astromech droids was busily repairing a Kuat *Corona*-class transport. On the third landing pad was a MandalMotors *Pursuer*-class enforcement ship, a thick, wedge-shaped vessel attached to a distinctive port-side outrigger that housed a powerful maneuvering thruster cluster.

A man clad in gray-and-blue segmented blast-resistant armor stood motionless beside the enforcement ship, waiting for Dooku. The man had a long-barreled sniper rifle slung over one shoulder, a pair of blaster pistols in cross-draw holsters on his belt, and a jetpack secured across his back. The jetpack was armed with an antivehicle homing missile. The man's head was completely obscured by a T-visored helmet, the distinctive mask of a Mandalorian warrior.

Seeing the Mandalorian, Dooku was reminded of a meeting on Kohlma that had occurred over a decade earlier, when he had recruited Jango Fett as the template for the now-thriving clone army. As Dooku recalled, it had been raining then, too.

Without breaking his stride, Dooku pushed his cape back, moved his hand to a leather pouch at his belt, and released three small silver orbs into the air. The orbs made simultaneous popping sounds as they burst through Dooku's personal energy field. Powered by miniature repulsorlift engines, each orb raced off in a different direction and rapidly ascended high into the rainy sky.

And then the orbs circled back, descending fast toward the Mandalorian. The armored man's gloved hands whipped to his belt and seized his pistols just as one orb opened fire. He ignored the incoming stream of energy bolts that whizzed past his form as he fired a single shot, his pistol making a barely audible *puff*. The first orb shattered in midair.

The second orb fired from behind. The Mandalorian spun on his left foot and dropped to a crouch as he raised his other pistol. Energy bolts tore into the ground where he had just been standing as he returned fire with another single shot. The orb exploded.

The third orb scored a glancing hit on the Mandalorian's shoulder plate as it sped straight toward him. The Mandalorian plunged his pistols back into their holsters, then reached for his rifle. Gripping the rifle's barrel, he swung hard at the approaching orb. The rifle's butt slammed into the orb, sending a spray of small metal bits across the landing pad.

"Impressive," Dooku said as he came to a stop before the Mandalorian. "You come highly recommended by your leader. I am grateful that he agreed to my request for assistance from the Death Watch, and I appreciate that you traveled to Kohlma so swiftly."

The Mandalorian slung his rifle back over his shoulder. His name was Hudu Shiv, but he had no reason to make introductions. "The Death Watch Command said you have an assignment for me." His low voice sounded like a restrained growl as it rattled through the filter of his helmet's built-in speaker.

Dooku drew a compact holoprojector from his pocket. He activated the holoprojector to display a three-dimensional image of a lean man with thinning hair. "Commissioner Langu Sommilor, a representative of Kynachi, is currently en route to a meeting with the Galactic Senate on Coruscant. My sources have informed me that Sommilor's ship will be refueling at the main spaceport on Vaced in approximately six standard hours." Dooku thumbed a switch on the holoprojector, and the hologram of Sommilor was replaced by an image of Sommilor's angular Suwantek Systems freighter. "Sommilor will rendezvous on Vaced with a Jedi who leads a squad of four Republic clone troopers." Dooku thumbed the switch again, and the hologram of the ship was replaced by the image of a blue-skinned boy with red eyes. "This Jedi, Nuru Kungurama, has been assigned to escort Sommilor to Coruscant."

Studying the hologram, Shiv said, "The Jedi is a child?"

"At any age, a Jedi is a Jedi," Dooku said. "Kungurama is not to be underestimated." He switched off the holoprojector and handed it to the warrior. "I have promised your leader that the day will soon come when the Death Watch will reclaim Mandalore from the cowards who have assumed power, and that you will have all the support of the Separatist forces. But for now, it is too soon to reveal the return of the Death Watch, or to allow the Galactic Senate to suspect a Mandalorian warrior is at large. Secrecy is essential to this assignment."

The Mandalorian did not waste words. "Who do you want me to kill?"

Dooku smiled. He told the Mandalorian exactly what he wanted done on Vaced. As he spoke, he handed Ambase's utility belt to the Mandalorian. When he was finished issuing instructions, he said, "Happy hunting." And then he turned and began walking back to his castle, taking his personal rain-deflector along with him.

The Mandalorian boarded his enforcement ship and sealed the hatch. Standing upon the airlock's grated floor, he hit a wall switch to activate a ring of decontamination nozzles that instantly spray-cleaned and dried his armor. He proceeded to the cockpit. Seconds later, the ship's engines ignited, sending a blast of steam into the rainfall behind the thrusters.

As the ship lifted off and ascended through the clouds, Shiv was confident that he would deliver death to Vaced.

CHAPTER 4

Overseer Umbrag's bulky Metalorn yacht dropped out of hyperspace at the outer edge of the Bilbringi system. The yacht's bow resembled a three-pronged fork. The rest of the vessel looked like a long box with blisters of automatic laser cannons. A moment after the yacht's arrival, six immense drone barges also exited hyperspace to materialize just behind the yacht.

"Scanning now," said one of the two droids at the navigational controls on the yacht's bridge. "No sign of any enemy vessels."

"Keep scanning for *any* vessels other than ours," said Umbrag from behind his breath mask. Clad in an armored pressure suit, the green-skinned humanoid Skakoan pushed himself out of his command seat and moved beside the droid pilot. His beady eyes squinted behind his metal-rimmed goggles as he peered through the main viewport. "Just look at all those asteroids out there. Must be thousands of them."

"Yes, sir," the pilot droid said.

Umbrag scowled. "I had everything under control on Kynachi until that Jedi brat came along."

"I know that you did, sir," the droid said sympathetically.

"And then, after I'd seized that space station at the edge of Wild Space, I was attacked by pirates!"

"I remember, sir," the droid said. "I was there, too."

"Count Dooku has assured me that we won't encounter any trouble at Bilbringi Depot, but I'm not taking any chances. The barges are carrying enough construction materials to build a small fleet of warships. The Techno Union can't afford to lose them."

"Of course not, sir."

"I just wish Dooku had sent more than twelve battle droids on this assignment."

"I do, too, sir."

"I don't know why I should have to wait a full week for reinforcements. Still no sign of any other vessels?"

"No, sir."

"Plot a course through the asteroid field."

"Yes, sir." The pilot extended an interface arm that he jacked into the yacht's navi-computer while his metal fingers tapped at other controls. Turning to his copilot, he said, "Direct the barges to follow our lead, and set the laser cannons for stray asteroids."

The copilot tapped at more controls. "Barges are set. Laser cannons ready."

Umbrag said, "Take us in."

The yacht moved into the asteroid field, trailed by the drone barges. As they headed toward the largest asteroid, two smaller asteroids with eccentric orbits tumbled toward the yacht. The laser cannons fired. As both asteroids were immediately reduced to space dust, the copilot cried out, "Take *that*, Republic dogs!"

The pilot droid looked at the copilot. "Those were asteroids, not Republic dogs."

"I know," said the copilot. "But if they had been

Republic dogs, I would have liked to blow them up just like that, and—"

"Quiet!" Umbrag roared.

Several minutes later, the yacht and barges arrived at Bilbringi Depot. Umbrag peered through the viewport to see the cluster of landing pads, modular structures, and docking bays that clung to the surface of the enormous asteroid. Although bright lights illuminated the landing and docking areas and evidenced that at least some of the depot's generators were running, there was no visible activity.

The pilot droid said, "The depot looks abandoned, sir."

"No, not abandoned," Umbrag said. "According to Count Dooku, it was, until recently, owned by a Hutt who donated it to the Separatist cause."

"Really?" said the droid. "I've never heard of a Hutt donating anything to anyone."

Umbrag sighed.

"Something wrong, sir?"

"I miss Kynachi," Umbrag said sadly. Raising his gloved hand, he made a fist. "If I ever get ahold of that meddlesome Jedi, I'll squeeze his neck until his blue head pops off."

"Watch your head, kid!" Gunn said as Nuru entered the *Hasty Harpy*'s cockpit. "Better buckle up. We're exiting hyperspace in five minutes."

Nuru belted himself into the rear seat behind Gunn and Chatterbox. Outside the cockpit's transparisteel windows, hyperspace appeared as a torrential cascade of brilliant lights. Gunn glanced back at Nuru and said, "When we leave hyperspace, we'll be broadcasting a fake transponder code. We don't want the *Harpy* to draw any unwanted attention in the Vaced system, so we'll show up on sensors as a merchant vessel from Coruscant."

"Sounds practical," Nuru said. "I just wish we could have found the hidden transmitter before we reached Vaced."

"Me too," Gunn said. "I hope I get my hands on whoever planted it!"

If whoever planted it doesn't get their hands on us first, Nuru thought. He watched Gunn and Chatterbox as they adjusted their instruments in preparation for the exit to real space. From what he could see, they appeared to have everything under control. *But that's what I thought before we wound up at the black hole.*

A few minutes later, the cascade of hyperspace washed away from the cockpit's view and was suddenly replaced by a starfield. Gunn checked the scopes, then tapped the controls to angle the *Harpy* toward the nearest planet, which was orbited by a single small moon. She said, "Welcome to the Vaced system."

Nuru noticed a few small starships in the distance, moving to and from the planet Vaced. He said, "Gunn, can your scanners determine if any of those vessels belong to the Techno Union or other Separatist factions?"

Gunn examined another scope. "Readings indicate they're just merchant ships and private cruisers."

"How do you know they're not using fake transponder codes like we are?"

"Kid, if they start shooting at us, I'll shoot back, okay? Now just sit back and leave the flying to me. The sooner we land, the sooner we can find that transmitter, meet the commissioner from Kynachi, and be on our way to Coruscant." Looking at Chatterbox, she added, "Unless, of course, we find romance on Vaced, in which case we might stay awhile."

Chatterbox muttered, "My heart's all aflutter."

Gunn chucked him in the shoulder. "You really don't know when to keep your mouth shut, do ya?!"

Nuru thought, *Gunn and Chatterbox certainly aren't behaving like sneaky saboteurs.* Once again, he found himself questioning Sharp's suspicions.

The *Harpy* was still traveling toward the green planet as another vessel dropped out of hyperspace into the Vaced system. The vessel was a MandalMotors *Pursuer*-class enforcement ship, and in its cockpit was the Mandalorian assassin Hudu Shiv.

CHAPTER 5

"Forget what I said about romance," Lalo Gunn said as she led Chatterbox and Nuru Kungurama down the *Hasty Harpy*'s boarding ramp. "This place is a dump."

Vaced Spaceport was a small sprawl of landing pads and a few ramshackle buildings, one of which appeared to be a trading post. Several workers and mechanics were visible. Nuru looked at the forested area beyond the spaceport. "I wouldn't call it a dump, Captain Gunn. The planet is remarkably beautiful in its own way, and the spaceport has a quaint charm."

Chatterbox, who was wearing a poncho to conceal his body armor, tapped Nuru's shoulder.

Nuru turned to see the clone glaring at him. "On second thought," Nuru added hastily, "the forests are probably filled with vicious creatures, and I suspect the spaceport has limited amenities. I admit I know little of romance, but I doubt anyone would ever find it here." He glanced at Chatterbox, who responded with an approving nod.

Gunn said, "Yeah? Well, you might change your tune about romance if you ran into Veeren again."

Veeren, also known as the Aristocra Sev'eere'nuruodo, an ambassador of the Chiss Ascendancy, was the first Chiss whom Nuru had ever met. Thinking of her, he felt his face flush a slightly deeper shade of blue.

"You don't have to listen to me, kid," Gunn continued. "But the way I see things, if you meet someone you like, you might as well tell them so. Otherwise, you might regret that you didn't say something when you had the chance."

Nuru was deciding whether he should respond to Gunn's comment when he was distracted by an unusual rumbling sound that came from beyond the spaceport's perimeter. He said, "What's that noise?"

"Swoops," Gunn said. "Sounds like a bunch of

'em." She looked at Nuru and Chatterbox. "Don't tell me you guys never heard of swoops before."

Nuru cocked his head. Chatterbox shrugged.

Gunn sighed. "A swoop bike is basically a repulsorlift engine with a seat on it, usually for a single rider."

Nuru said, "Like a speeder bike?"

"Bigger and faster. Way more powerful. Definitely not for kids."

"I wasn't thinking of riding one any time soon," Nuru said. "We need to find the transmitter before Commissioner Sommilor arrives. I'll be right back."

Nuru went back up the *Harpy*'s boarding ramp. He found Breaker, Sharp, Knuckles, and Cleaver in the main hold. Like Chatterbox, the other clones were not wearing their helmets and had ponchos draped over their armor, and Cleaver had wriggled into a hooded robe. Nuru had instructed all the members of Breakout Squad to cover up because they did not want to attract any attention from the local population. To diminish the clones' resemblance, Knuckles and Breaker wore different colored caps, and Sharp had a set of goggles strapped across his forehead.

Breaker said, "Is it all right for us to go outside, Commander?"

"Yes," Nuru replied. "But we must exercise caution. Breaker, you and I will be lookouts while everyone else searches the hull for the transmitter."

Sharp said, "Begging your pardon, Commander, but perhaps I should be a lookout? I have sharp eyesight. That's how I got my nickname, you know."

Nuru smiled politely as Sharp had mentioned the origin of his nickname more than once. "Thank you, Sharp, but finding the transmitter may require keen vision, too."

"As you wish, Commander," Sharp replied.

Knuckles and Breaker walked out of the hold with Cleaver right behind them. Sharp stepped beside Nuru and whispered, "Commander, are you sure you wouldn't rather have me accompany you as a lookout? Until we identify the saboteur, we shouldn't take any—"

"I'll be all right," Nuru said. "I'm trusting you to keep those sharp eyes of yours on everyone else."

"Very good, sir."

Sharp and Nuru stepped outside. They found the others standing on the landing pad beside the

Harpy. Knuckles stretched. "Feels good to breathe fresh air for a change, doesn't it?"

"Sure does," Breaker said.

"I wouldn't know," Cleaver added. "I don't breathe."

Knuckles cast a glance at Sharp and said, "I think *some* of us prefer filtered air, at least while sleeping. Isn't that right, Sharp?" Knuckles laughed.

Sharp grinned and turned to Nuru. "Knuckles is just joking with me. I've gotten into the habit of sleeping with my helmet on. It helps muffle the noise of the *Harpy*'s engines."

Knuckles said, "Every time I've ever fallen asleep while wearing my helmet, I wake up with a stiff neck."

"Cut the chatter," Gunn called out. "Let's find that rotten transmitter." She lowered an extendible maintenance ladder that stretched to the *Harpy*'s upper hull. Chatterbox and Cleaver followed Gunn up the ladder while Sharp and Knuckles began searching for the transmitter on the lower hull.

As Nuru and Breaker walked slowly around the ship, Breaker said, "Any idea what we might be looking out for, Commander?"

"Not really," Nuru said as they walked past a neighboring landing pad where an Arcona mechanic with an anvil-shaped head was working on his courier ship. "Anything resembling trouble, I guess."

Breaker glanced over his shoulder to make sure the other members of Breakout Squad would not be able to hear him. He whispered, "Permission to speak freely, Commander?"

"Yes, of course."

"It's about the activation of the *Harpy*'s hyperspace transponder. The thing is, I'm certain I didn't do it, sir. And it's not exactly easy to switch it on accidentally."

He's sounding like Sharp, Nuru thought with some alarm. He whispered in return, "You're suggesting someone activated it deliberately?"

"I don't know, sir. But Sharp was helping me with the systems check, and . . . Commander, have you noticed anything odd about Sharp?"

Nuru considered telling Breaker about Sharp's suspicions of a saboteur on the *Harpy*, but decided against it. He replied, "Why do you ask?"

"Lately, he seems . . . well, guarded. And every few days, he reminds us all about his 'sharp eyesight.'

Chatterbox and I were with him when Captain Lock nicknamed him Sharp. It's not as if we would forget."

"I did notice Sharp has mentioned his eyesight more than once, but I didn't think much of it."

"Just the same," Breaker added. "I'm concerned. When we get back to Coruscant, I'll recommend he consults a clone counselor, just to make sure everything is all right with—"

Rumbling noises came from beyond the wooded area next to the spaceport. Turning to face the tall trees, Breaker said, "Sounds like repulsorlift engines."

"Gunn told me they're swoop bikes."

And then five swoops tore into view, launching away from a cluster of trees at the edge of the woods. Even across the distance, Nuru could see that the biker on the rearmost swoop was an unusually large humanoid.

The five swoops angled toward the spaceport, and then the leader gunned his engine and veered off toward the *Harpy*'s landing pad. The other bikers followed.

On top of the *Harpy*, Gunn saw the swoops and said, "Heads up, fellas." The other members of Breakout Squad paused in their search for the transmitter and directed their attention to the incoming bikers.

Stepping in front of Nuru, Breaker reached under his poncho to unholster his blaster pistol. Nuru said, "Stay calm, Breaker. They may be harmless."

The five bikers came to a stop and killed their engines at the edge of the landing pad. All the bikers had holstered blasters at their belts. The lead biker wore a helmet with a large, sharp-tipped horn that extended above his visor. He pulled off the helmet to reveal it had a hole above the visor, and that the horn was actually part of his own hairless head. The biker had muddy-yellow skin and big black eyes. Nuru recognized the alien biker's species as an Advozse.

Three other bikers removed their helmets to reveal themselves as human males with unshaven faces. The monstrous biker on the rearmost swoop was the only one not wearing a helmet, but Nuru imagined few manufacturers made helmets for heads so large. The giant had orange skin and long, pointed ears that jutted out beside his head, and he wore a vest over his shirtless torso, exposing a mountainous mass of muscle. Dirty black hair sprouted from his cranium, and a large gold ring dangled below his nostrils. Nuru did not recognize the giant's species and suspected he was a hybrid, possibly a mix of human and Moggonite.

The giant swung his bulk off his swoop, which adjusted to the loss of weight by ascending several centimeters before it leveled off. Nuru guessed he was at least two meters tall. The giant faced Nuru and grinned, revealing a lot of sharp teeth.

The other bikers remained on their swoops. The Advozse blinked his black eyes at Breaker and said, "Welcome to Vaced, stranger. I'm Frutchoo. I represent the law around here, and these are my deputies."

The giant muttered, "You *know* I don't like being called your deputy, Frutchoo. Nobody bosses me around."

"Pardon me," Frutchoo said. "I meant to say my *associates*."

Breaker said, "Nice of you to greet us."

The giant yawned. "Can we get this over with? I wanna go get a drink."

"You *always* want to get a drink," said one of the human bikers. "You're a regular fozbeer fiend."

The giant reached out with one hand, grabbed

the other biker by the collar, lifted him off the swoop, and snarled, "You got somethin' against fozbeer?"

The biker gasped, "No!"

"Good," said the giant. He released his grip. The biker landed hard upon his swoop's saddle.

Ignoring his allies, Frutchoo continued, "It's my duty to collect the spaceport tax from all new arrivals. The tax is kind of like insurance. It prevents anything bad from happening to your ship." He pointed to the nearby Arcona mechanic. "That guy probably wouldn't be fixing a thruster plate right now if he'd paid the tax."

Overhearing this, the Arcona sputtered with outrage, "I *did* pay the tax!"

"Not fast enough," Frutchoo said with a shrug.

Nuru smiled. "You don't want anyone to pay the spaceport tax."

Frutchoo shook his head and said, "I don't want anyone to pay the spaceport tax."

Nuru glanced at the giant and remembered what he had said about wanting a drink. Nuru said, "You're *all* very thirsty."

The other bikers cleared their throats while the giant dragged a massive, hairy arm across his suddenly parched lips. Frutchoo made a rasping sound, then said, "We're all very thirsty."

"You should find a nice, quiet place for a drink."

Frutchoo turned to the other bikers and said, "Let's go to the tavern for some drinks."

Nuru added, "You're buying."

"I'm buying." Frutchoo put his helmet back on, and then he and the giant climbed back onto their swoops. All the bikers gunned their engines, then Frutchoo led them back toward the trading post.

Breaker grinned. He had witnessed Nuru's skill with Jedi mind tricks before. As the swoop gang parked their swoops outside the trading post, which evidently had a tavern on the premises, Breaker said, "Well done, Commander."

A gust of wind blew in from over the grassy plain. As the breeze rustled through the leaves of the trees in the woods beside the spaceport, Breaker said, "I just had a nasty thought."

"What is it?"

"Those trees over there are the highest things in the area, the only things that overlook our position. A good vantage point for anyone who wanted to keep an eye on us. Maybe I should go take a look?"

"Good thinking," Nuru said. "But take your helmet and rifle." Patting the comlink that was clipped beside the two lightsabers on his belt, he added, "Contact me if you see anything unusual or need help."

"Yes, sir."

Breaker went back into the *Harpy* and exited a moment later, carrying his helmet and blaster rifle. Seeing him, Nuru said, "On second thought, contact me when you reach the trees."

"You're worried about me?"

"I'm concerned about us all."

Breaker put on his helmet. "Talk with you soon, sir." He walked off, heading for the field of tall grass that lay between the spaceport and the forest.

Nuru looked at Knuckles and Sharp, who were both so busy searching for the transmitter on the *Harpy*'s belly that they had not noticed Breaker's departure. Nuru considered telling Sharp to go along with Breaker, but when he looked back to the grassy field, Breaker had already vanished.

Hudu Shiv landed his enforcement ship in the shadow of a craggy cliff, six kilometers west of Vaced Spaceport. Looking through the cockpit window, he saw the surrounding rocks were weirdly cylindrical and colorful. He realized he had touched down in the remains of an ancient petrified forest. Except for a small cloud of insects several meters away from the ship, there was no sign of life.

Shiv had already attached the leather utility belt that Dooku had given him to his own belt. Leaving the cockpit, he secured his rifle across his shoulder as he moved past the hatch for the ship's emergency lifeboat. He went to the cargo hold, where a sleek speeder bike was racked against a bulkhead. The bike appeared to be a standard Mobquet Ripper with a powerful repulsorlift engine and front-mounted steering vanes, but the engine was armor-plated and the steering vanes had been filed to razor sharpness. The bike also carried a small arsenal of concealed weapons as well as a supply pack that held a set of tree-climbing spurs.

Moving methodically, Shiv unlocked the bike, pulled it away from the bulkhead, and used his elbow to press a button to open the cargo hatch as he climbed onto the bike. The hatch opened with a hissing sound. He kicked off with his legs, allowing the bike to glide silently out of the ship. Once outside, he tapped a remote to secure the ship and then launched his bike away from his landing site.

The surrounding rocks suddenly blurred past Shiv's bike. Less than a minute later, he was skimming over the grassy plain, heading for the forest near the spaceport. Behind his helmet, his steely eyes glanced at a time display. If Count Dooku's intelligence sources were correct, Commissioner Sommilor's ship would arrive on Vaced in less than an hour.

Shiv accelerated. He ignored the rush of air against his armored shoulders and blocked out the whine of the speeder bike's engine. Calming his mind, he visualized what would happen next.

He would reach the forest. He would park the speeder bike near the base of a tall tree. He would climb the tree, taking his rifle with him. He would watch the skies for Sommilor's starship and wait for it to land at the spaceport.

And then the killing would begin.

CHAPTER 6

Boom.

Ring-Sol Ambase opened his eyes. *Was that thunder?*

Still lying on the bed that was surrounded by medical computers, Ambase looked to the single window in his chamber, trying to determine whether the gray sky had grown darker.

How long was I unconscious? He remembered the droids had escorted the clone trooper out of his chamber. He did not recall drifting off into a dreamless sleep, or—

Boom. KaBOOM.

Ambase's body went rigid. *That's not thunder.*

More explosions followed, each growing louder than the last. Ambase thought they sounded like cluster bombs. As another series of explosions shook the walls and knocked the medical equipment to the floor, he took a deep breath and tried to elevate his head and shoulders. One of the diagnostic computers began beeping loudly.

As more blasts wracked the building, three B1 battle droids, each carrying an E-5 blaster rifle, stumbled through the doorway into Ambase's chamber. Two droids began hastily gathering the medical equipment. The third droid grabbed a metal bar at the foot of Ambase's bed and yanked it, hauling the bed toward the doorway. As the bed moved across the room without any indication of friction against the floor, Ambase realized his bed rested upon a hovering gravsled.

"What's happening?" Ambase said. "Who's attacking the—?"

From the bed, Ambase watched in amazement as the clone who claimed to be Sharp—still clad in the gray clothes Dooku had given him—dived head first through the doorway and into the chamber. One droid opened fire, missing the clone but blasting a hole near the base of one wall. The clone somersaulted and came to a stop in a low crouch. He was holding a blaster rifle. He fired, cutting down two droids instantly.

The remaining droid returned fire. The clone jumped sideways to dodge the blaster bolts, then kicked off one wall and launched himself at the droid.

The clone slammed against the droid's body, causing the droid to stumble backward. Unprepared for the assault, the droid fired reflexively and accidentally blasted the transparisteel window behind him. The window exploded outward, and a cold wind whipped into the chamber. The droid tripped over his feet and fell back against the ruined window's frame.

Moving fast, the clone braced one of his own legs behind the droid's left ankle as he shoved the droid hard. The shove carried the droid through the window, and then the droid was gone.

Ambase gasped. "How did you—?"

"No time to talk, sir." The clone stepped over the ruined droids, seized the metal bar at the foot of the bed, and pulled the gravsled after him through the doorway.

More explosions sounded outside the building as the clone hauled the gravsled through a corridor. Ambase saw dust falling from the ceiling and squeezed his eyes shut. He said, "Where's Dooku?"

"I think he went to his sailer." More blasts wracked the building. Ambase opened his eyes to see the clone was heading for a closed door. The clone used his elbow to strike a metal panel on the wall, and the door slid open.

The clone hauled him through the doorway. Ambase smelled cold, wet air mixed with fire and smoke. Ambase's eyes began to tear. He held his breath and closed his eyes again. He felt rain pelt his face and heard the roar of starfighters overhead. Recognizing the noise of the engines, he gasped out, "Republic starfighters?"

"Sounds like it, sir."

When they emerged from the smoke, Ambase opened his eyes and saw that the clone had delivered them to a staggered series of landing pads. Ambase realized the pads were the ones that the clone had mentioned earlier while looking out the window from the medical chamber. The clone had claimed he had seen three ships, but Ambase saw only two.

One was a needle-nosed, ridged-back Kuat *Corona*-class transport, which showed no obvious sign of damage. The other was a blazing wreck, but Ambase could make out that it was a seed-shaped vessel with two long, forward prongs jutting above and below a bubble cockpit, which was now shattered and expelling gas and smoke. Ambase immediately recognized the wreckage.

Dooku's solar sailer! Is Dooku . . . dead?!

The Kuat transport's hatch was already open. The clone shoved the gravsled that carried Ambase through the Kuat transport's open hatch, and then secured the gravsled to a bulkhead behind the cockpit. Blaster fire began hammering at the transport's exterior. The clone jumped into the cockpit and began throwing switches.

Ambase said, "You can fly this?"

"Yes, sir."

Ambase heard the engines fire, and then the transport lifted off. Rain pounded at the hull, and the entire ship shuddered as it rose up through gray clouds. Twisting his head, Ambase could see the clone in the cockpit, wrestling with the flight controls.

Laser fire tore at the transport's shields. Ambase

said, "Who's shooting at us?"

"The scopes read twelve Delta-7Bs. I can't see them through these clouds."

Startled, Ambase said, "Twelve . . . Jedi starfighters?!"

"They think we're the enemy! I'm trying to hail them." Another explosion caused the transport to lurch hard to port. "The comm's not working. I can't—"

"Just get us out of here!"

The clone took evasive action, sending the transport hard to the side, then arcing straight up. They broke through the clouds, and a field of stars came into view. As they hurtled into space, Ambase said, "Are we being followed?"

"No, sir. Scopes indicate the starfighters stayed behind to hammer Dooku's castle." The clone adjusted one of the scopes.

"Tell me . . . how did you get out of your cell?"

"I overheard Dooku telling the droids that Republic ships were incoming. He told the droids to bring you and me to his solar sailer. Two droids were escorting me from my cell when I decided to make a break for it. I got lucky."

Ambase's mind raced. "Do you know if Dooku survived?"

"No, sir. But if he made it into his sailer before it got hit, I doubt he could have lived."

Even though Ambase was still weak, he suspected he would have sensed Dooku's death. He took a deep breath. "Can you confirm we're in the Bogden system?"

The clone checked a navigational console. "Readings indicate we just left Kohlma, one of Bogden's moons. Our hyperdrive appears to be operational. Should I set the navi-computer to plot a course for Coruscant?"

Ambase suddenly recalled what Dooku had said about the possibility of the Sith turning Jedi apprentices against their own Masters. "No. I need time to recover . . . and think." He remembered Dooku's claim that Nuru had seized Bilbringi Depot. Although he had no reason to believe Dooku, he felt compelled to investigate. He said, "Can you get us to the Bilbringi system?"

The clone consulted the nav console again. "Yes, sir, but . . . it will take a while."

"Do it."

Count Dooku stood outside his castle and watched the astromech droids extinguish the flames from the apparently ruined solar sailer. In fact, the wreckage had been originally nothing more than a full-scale, nonworking replica. His actual ship had been moved to a hangar on the other side of the castle.

Thanks to the falling rain, the fire-fighting astromechs accomplished their job quickly. When they were done, Dooku directed their attention to the castle's entrance and said, "There are wrecked droids inside the castle. Gather all of their parts and bring them to the recycler." One astromech beeped in response, then the others followed him away from the smoldering replica.

The sound of Jedi starfighters circling overhead did not alarm Dooku, for the noise, like the replica solar sailer, was a ruse of his invention. He looked up to see Asajj Ventress's Fanblade starfighter descend to the landing pad that had been previously occupied by the Kuat transport. Hovering alongside Ventress's fighter were eleven small, silver orbs.

Ventress exited her fighter and spotted Dooku standing below his personal floating energy shield. "The transport fled into space," she said. "If the smoke bombs and flash detonators weren't enough to convince those two fools that Republic forces were attacking your castle, seeing twelve 'Jedi starfighters' on their scopes certainly did the job."

Dooku glanced at the floating orbs. Like Ventress's Fanblade, each orb had been rigged to transmit a signal that would make them appear as Delta-7Bs on enemy scopes. Dooku said, "Remove the fake transponder codes from your fighter and the remotes, then meet me inside the communications chamber."

Dooku started to walk away, but Ventress said, "Wait. I don't like being kept in the dark. Tell me, Master . . . why did you have me bring Ambase and that clone all the way from Kynachi, only to let them escape?"

Dooku smiled. "If you ever had any reservations about working in darkness, Ventress, you never should have offered your services to me." And then Dooku turned and walked back to his castle, leaving Ventress quietly fuming in the rain.

CHAPTER 7

"I've found something," Cleaver said. Standing with Lalo Gunn and Chatterbox atop the *Hasty Harpy*, the droid held out a small, weathered strip of metal with a clamping mechanism on one end. "It was stuck along the upper edge of a heat vent. Could it be the transmitter?"

Gunn said, "*That* is a durasteel patch, and the only thing it's transmitting is your lack of brain waves. Put it back where you found it and keep looking."

"Yes, Captain."

On the landing pad, in the *Harpy*'s shadow, Nuru Kungurama walked quietly back and forth.

He was alternately watching the perimeter of Vaced Spaceport and the sky overhead. He glanced at Knuckles and Sharp, who were still busy searching every nook of the *Harpy*'s belly for the mysterious transmitter.

Sharp moved away from one of the *Harpy*'s landing legs. Looking past Nuru, he said, "Where's Breaker?"

"He went to look around over there," Nuru said, gesturing to the tall trees at the edge of the wooded area beside the spaceport.

Sharp stepped closer to Nuru. Lowering his voice so Knuckles could not hear, he said, "Commander, I'm not sure that was a good idea. So long as Breaker is a suspect, he shouldn't be allowed to—"

"I trust him, Sharp," Nuru interrupted. Keeping his own voice low, he continued, "I realize there may be a saboteur among us, but I trust Breaker just as much as I trust you." He looked again to the forest. "If anyone *is* watching us, we wouldn't want to find out the hard way."

"No, sir," Sharp said. "That we wouldn't."

Breaker moved quietly and kept low, making sure his helmet never poked above the high grass that grew at the edge of the forest. He could still hear the noises of workers and a few vehicles from the spaceport, which was now nearly half a kilometer behind him. Moving up a low slope, he held his rifle ready and kept his eyes on the trees ahead.

Snap.

Breaker stopped and swung his rifle to his right to see what had made the sound. He saw a group of medium-sized reptavians with shimmering green-and-blue scales around their long, unfeathered necks. One reptavian had just broken a twig that it was adding to its nest. The reptavians glanced at Breaker, then looked away, apparently disinterested.

Breaker pressed on, moving through the grass until he arrived at a cluster of tall trees. Listening carefully, he realized the noises from the spaceport had become less distinct. He stepped cautiously around the wide trunk of one tree and let his helmet's optical sensors adjust to the shadowy forest floor.

Something moved to his upper left, and Breaker instinctively took aim with his rifle. He found himself staring at a pair of reptiles that were slithering around the lower limbs of the nearest tree. The lizards' dark leathery skin blended almost perfectly with the tree's bark. Breaker lowered his rifle but kept his finger close to the trigger.

He moved between the trees to a rise that offered a clear view of the spaceport. He was able to easily pick out the *Hasty Harpy* from the other ships across the distance, and he could also see a few small specks that he knew were actually people near the trading post. Activating his helmet's built-in comlink, he said, "Breaker to Kungurama, do you read me?"

A moment later, Nuru's voice responded, "I read you, Breaker. Find anything interesting?"

"Just flora and fauna. But I'm still looking."

"Keep me posted."

Breaker turned off his comlink and looked around his position. Knowing his view of the spaceport would be better from a higher elevation, he tilted his head back and looked up to study the thickness and location of the branches that weaved between the trees. He was still plotting his climb to one particular branch when he noticed what appeared to be a gouge in the bark of one tree, just below a freshly broken branch.

The gouge looked as if it had been made by the heel of a boot.

Breaker backed up, carefully and silently. Keeping his rifle leveled at the tree in front of him, he looked up and down, searching for any sign of the person, creature, or droid that must have stepped on the branch and broken it.

As he moved backward, he was surprised to bump into something behind him. He spun around to see he had struck a speeder bike that was parked at a dead hover above the ground.

And then something hit Breaker hard against the back of his helmet and everything went dark.

Hudu Shiv hung upside down, his jetpack's missile aimed at the ground. He peered through his helmet's visor and watched the clone trooper fall. Still mostly concealed by a Mandalorian camouflage net, he had his legs wrapped around a strong branch that extended directly above the trooper. His boots were outfitted with the tree-climbing spurs he had brought from his ship.

Two minutes earlier, Shiv had been halfway up the tree when he had spotted the top of the trooper's helmet moving through the high grass near a bunch of reptavians at the edge of the forest. Shiv had then descended to his current position, concealed himself with the camo net, dangled from the branch, and waited for the trooper to move beneath him. When that moment came, he had used his rifle's butt to bring the trooper down with a single blow.

Clutching his rifle, Shiv swung down from the branch and landed between the parked speeder bike and the unconscious trooper's crumpled body. He brushed back the camo net so it was draped over one shoulder, slung his rifle over his back, then bent down and pulled off the trooper's helmet.

Although members of the Death Watch had become aware of the origins of the Republic's clone army, Shiv found himself impressed by the unmasked clone's remarkable resemblance to Jango Fett. Shiv had known Fett, and from what he could see, the only physical difference was that Fett's face had been heavily scarred.

Shiv placed the trooper's helmet on the ground. He could see the clone was still breathing.

Dooku's instructions had been very specific: Shiv was to refrain from killing anyone until after the ship from Kynachi arrived on Vaced, and he was to leave Vaced without being seen. And so he reached to his belt, uncoiled a long, thin strand of plastifiber, and quickly bound the trooper's wrists and ankles. Tearing off a length of the camo net, he wrapped it tightly across the clone's mouth, gagging him, and then continued wrapping it around the clone's eyes. He shoved the clone up against a tree and used another strand of plastifiber to tie him to the trunk.

He picked up the trooper's helmet, looked inside it, and saw the embedded comlink. Not wanting to waste precious time prying out the comlink, he tucked the entire helmet into his camo net, then moved past his speeder bike and went to the tree that he had already selected as his firing point. As sturdy as it was tall, the tree's upper branches swayed only slightly, not enough to pose any problems for a sniper of Shiv's caliber. Although his jetpack could have carried him swiftly to the top of the tree, the jets would have been visible from the spaceport. He dug his spurs into the tree's bark and scurried upward.

Arriving at his perch, Shiv strapped himself to a

thick bough. He removed the trooper's helmet from the camo net and jammed it over some twigs that jutted out from a branch near his own head.

Shiv looked down at the grassy field that stretched out below the trees. He spotted the reptavians, still at rest. He hoped they would remain where they were for a while yet.

He unslung his rifle and popped its retractable targeting scope. The electronic scope transmitted visual data directly to an optical sensor inside his T-visor, enabling him to clearly see the scope's focal point without removing his helmet. He braced the stock up against his right shoulder and let the rifle's barrel rest upon another branch to steady his aim. Shiv shifted the rifle slowly, letting it pivot on the branch as he searched for the ship that had delivered the clone trooper to Vaced.

Sweeping the scope from ship to ship, Shiv passed over an Arcona who appeared to be mending a thruster plate on an old courier, and then spied a man who wore a poncho and was kneeling atop a Corellian YT-1760 transport. The man turned his head. Shiv saw his face was identical to the captive clone's.

Two more figures became visible atop the Corellian transport. Much to Hudu Shiv's surprise, one was a Separatist BX-series droid commando. The other was a human female.

Behind his helmet's visor, Shiv scowled. Count Dooku had not mentioned anything about a droid commando. Shiv wondered if Dooku had known about the droid, or if there were anything else that the Separatist leader had failed to tell him.

Shifting the scope, Shiv saw two more clone troopers moving beneath the transport. And then he saw a third figure, standing on the ground near the boarding ramp: a young blue-skinned boy he recognized immediately from the hologram that Dooku had shown him. The boy was Nuru Kungurama, the Jedi.

Shiv took a deep breath and then exhaled slowly. His education had included history lessons about Mandalorian encounters with the Jedi, and he knew it was best if he remained calm. Jedi were notorious for their ability to detect powerful emotions. Some scholars maintained a Jedi could sense an enemy's anxiety and rage as easily as a microbarometer could measure atmospheric pressure.

Increasing the targeting scope's magnification, Shiv zoomed in on Kungurama's head. The boy turned and looked toward the forest, his red eyes drifting until he seemed to be looking directly at Shiv. The sniper did not panic, and his index finger, already curled around his rifle's trigger, did not twitch. The boy's gaze drifted again, and then he tilted his head back to gaze skyward.

Keeping Kungurama's head at the very center of the scope's crosshairs, Shiv licked his upper lip. He would not deny he was tempted to squeeze the trigger, but he was obliged to obey Dooku's instructions. It was a matter of honor.

A sound caught Shiv's attention. Without moving his rifle, he lifted his gaze to the sky to follow Kungurama's gaze at an incoming ship—a Suwantek Systems TL-1800 freighter. Evidently, the commissioner from Kynachi was arriving right on schedule.

Shiv did not take any pleasure from killing. As a Death Watch assassin, taking lives was simply what he did, and what he did best. Still, as the TL-1800 flew toward the spaceport, he did find himself pleased with the progress of his current assignment.

He liked it when his targets were punctual.

"Heads up, fellas," Lalo Gunn said from atop the *Hasty Harpy*, where she stood near Chatterbox and Cleaver. Chatterbox looked up to see the TL-1800 freighter descending to Vaced Spaceport.

Cleaver rose from a section of hull behind the *Harpy*'s cockpit. Holding up a small gray cylinder with a magnetic strip on the side and a single black metal rod sticking out of one end, he said, "I've found something."

"Save it for later, Cleaver," Gunn said as she moved to the edge of the ship.

"But I think—"

"Not now!" While Cleaver continued to study the gray cylinder, Gunn leaned out over the side of the ship and called out, "Hey, kid! The commissioner's ship is coming in!"

Nuru stood on the landing pad near the *Harpy*'s boarding ramp. He had already heard and spotted the ship, which now hovered over a vacant landing pad just beyond the Arcona's courier ship. Knuckles and Sharp stepped out from under the *Harpy* and moved up beside Nuru.

"I should alert Breaker," Nuru said. He activated his comlink. "Nuru to Breaker, do you read me?"

Through his rifle scope, the Mandalorian saw Kungurama speaking into the comlink at the same time that he heard the boy's voice emit from the helmet he had taken from the knocked-out trooper. Keeping his right hand gripped on the rifle and his eye on the scope, Shiv reached into the trooper's helmet and dragged his gloved fingers back and forth across the embedded comlink. He spoke in short, fragmented bursts. "Barely hear . . . is fine but . . . interference in . . . maybe trees." Then he stopped talking but continued scratching the comlink, waiting for the boy's response.

"What's wrong with Breaker's voice?" Knuckles said.

"Too much static," Sharp said. "Sounded like he said maybe the trees are causing interference."

"Quiet," Nuru said as he adjusted the comlink. "Breaker, if you can hear me, return to the spaceport. The ship from Kynachi has arrived." He returned the comlink to his belt.

Nuru took a few steps away from the *Harpy*, then turned and looked up to see Gunn, Chatterbox, and Cleaver on the upper hull. "I sent Breaker to

85 ///

scout the woods, but something's interfering with our comlinks. You three stay here and watch the perimeter, see if you can spot him while the rest of us greet the commissioner."

Gunn said, "Say *please*."

"Please, Captain Gunn."

"Okay."

Nuru led Sharp and Knuckles around the Arcona's pad, but stopped short of the next one, where the TL-1800's landing jets were kicking up a circle of dust. The ship's articulated legs were still settling onto the ground as a hatch opened on the port side and then a boarding ramp extended.

Shiv could not have anticipated which landing pad the TL-1800 would touch down upon, or which way its boarding hatches would be facing. From what he could see, Kungurama and two clones faced the ship's extended boarding ramp. He could not see the hatch that he knew must be at the top of the ramp, but a moment later, he saw two men step down toward Kungurama.

Two broad-shouldered pilots in green uniforms exited the TL-1800's hatch and descended the ramp. Nuru noticed KynachTech insignias on their tunics. The ship's engines were still winding down as Langu Sommilor stepped out after the pilots. Sommilor smiled. Raising his voice so he could be heard over the engines, he said, "Nuru Kungurama, I presume?"

Shiv watched the two men lead Sommilor down the ramp. He expected Kungurama would bow his head in greeting to Sommilor and was not surprised when the Jedi did just that. Kungurama had just lowered his head as Shiv thumbed his rifle's ammo-select button and quickly shifted the weapon down and to the side. The resting reptavians appeared in his scope. He squeezed the trigger.

His selected projectile was an explosive compressed-air pellet. It smashed into the ground between the reptavians and detonated with a quiet pop that sent a blast of air in all directions.

As the alarmed but unharmed creatures screeched and took flight, Shiv had already thumbed the ammo-select button again and swung his rifle back toward Sommilor's ship, just in time to view

Kungurama, through the scope, lift his head to face Sommilor.

Facing Sommilor, Nuru was momentarily distracted by a flock of reptavians that rose from the field before the forest. He wondered if Breaker had stumbled upon the creatures' nesting grounds.

Shiv locked his target in the scope's crosshairs. He exhaled. He squeezed the trigger. This time, his selected projectiles were not compressed-air pellets.

CHAPTER 8

Standing before Nuru at the bottom of the TL-1800's boarding ramp, Commissioner Sommilor winced as he reached up and slapped the back of his own neck. For a moment, Nuru thought the man had been stung by an insect, but then Sommilor gasped and fell to his knees.

Nuru took a quick step forward to catch Sommilor, wrapping his arms around the man's torso to hold him upright. Sharp, Knuckles, and the two KynachTech pilots leaned in as Sommilor's head lolled onto Nuru's shoulder. Sharp said, "Did he faint?"

Nuru moved his hand up behind Sommilor's

neck and felt a tiny object sticking out. He plucked the object out and held it up for inspection. It was a dart, its sharp tip smeared with blood.

"Sniper," Sharp said as he swung his blaster rifle out from under his poncho and jumped beside Nuru and Sommilor, positioning his own body as a shield to protect the others.

Knuckles was already brandishing his rifle. Looking at the two KynachTech pilots, he said, "Take cover!" Before either pilot could obey the command, one slapped at the side of his own neck, and then the other did the same. Both men gasped and collapsed.

"Help them!" Nuru said urgently as he shuffled backward, hauling Sommilor with him. He wanted to draw his lightsaber, but he needed both hands to drag Sommilor to safety. While Knuckles and Sharp grabbed the two fallen pilots, Nuru reprimanded himself for having been temporarily distracted by the reptavians that had taken flight a moment before Sommilor had been hit. He did not pause to check Sommilor's pulse as he shoved the man's body under the boarding ramp.

Staying close to the side of the ship, Nuru drew his lightsaber, ignited its blue blade, and prepared to strike any more incoming darts. Because the Arcona's courier ship blocked his view of the *Hasty Harpy*, he did not know whether Chatterbox, Gunn, and Cleaver were aware of the attack. With his free hand, he activated his comlink and said, "Chatterbox! Get everyone off the top of the *Harpy*. A sniper hit the Kynachi landing party."

Nuru looked away from the ship, visually calculating the darts' firing point to the high trees at the edge of the forest. And then he remembered . . .

Breaker?! Nuru felt suddenly queasy.

Sharp moved close to Nuru and said, "Keep your head down, Commander!"

Has Breaker been killed? Or did he *fire the darts?* Nuru felt overwhelmed and unsure of what to do next. He took a breath and relaxed his mind.

"Commander, please step back to the—"

Nuru deactivated his lightsaber. "Secure the perimeter and don't let anyone else get hurt," he said quickly. "I'm going after the sniper."

Sharp started to protest, but Nuru was already sprinting away from the TL-1800, heading for the trading post. Although his Jedi powers enabled him to run faster than ordinary humanoids, Nuru knew that he might not reach the forest in time to stop the sniper from escaping, especially if the sniper had a transport. He ran a zigzag path past the landing pads until he arrived at the swoops parked outside the trading post.

Nuru did not waste any time selecting a vehicle. He jumped onto the saddle of the nearest swoop. In less than a second, he assessed that the controls were not very different from the speeder bikes used for training exercises at the Jedi Temple. Unfortunately, the swoop's customized handlebar controllers were beyond his grasp. He realized he had landed on the swoop that belonged to the orange-skinned giant.

"Hey!" someone roared behind Nuru. He glanced over his shoulder to see the giant himself, stepping away from a tree outside the trading post. "Get offa my bike!"

Nuru leaped onto a smaller swoop and seized the controllers without difficulty. "I'm just borrowing this," he said before he punched the ignition.

He gunned the engine, then zoomed away from the trading post. Unprepared for the swoop's incredible velocity, he tightened his grip on the handlebars and had to press his thighs against the saddle to keep his legs from flying out from under him. Within seconds, he was racing over the grassy field that lay between the spaceport and the forest.

Just as he had sprinted across the spaceport, Nuru cut a zigzag path over the field. He believed weaving from side to side was the best way to avoid making himself an easy target.

But then he swerved too hard. The swoop went into an unexpected half roll that carried him upside down. Blades of grass whipped at his inverted head as he hurtled forward. He adjusted his grip on one of the handlebars, and the swoop completed its roll so he was once again upright. No sooner had he regained control of the swoop when he sensed movement behind him. He risked a quick look back.

Four swoops were tearing away from the spaceport, racing after him. Frutchoo and the giant were in the lead, followed by the human bikers, two of whom were seated on a single swoop. Nuru realized the giant must have alerted the other members of the gang, who were swerving wildly. He suspected they were so angry they couldn't steer straight.

He doubted Frutchoo's gang had any interest in his reasons for taking one of their swoops.

Hudu Shiv brought the Republic trooper's helmet with him as he climbed down the tree. During his descent, he saw Nuru Kungurama run to the trading post and take a swoop, and now, as he walked toward his own speeder bike, he could hear the swoop's engine getting increasingly louder as it approached the forest. He glanced at the tree trunk where he had left the clone, who remained bound and motionless.

Reaching to his own belt, Shiv unclasped the leather utility belt that Dooku had given him. He tossed the belt down so it fell beside the clone's body, where it would be easily found.

Shiv heard more swoops roaring across the distance. He trotted past his speeder bike and moved around a tree to see Kungurama steering a swoop low over the grassy field with four swoops coming up fast behind him.

Shiv considered Count Dooku's orders. He was not about to let the swoop gang interfere with the mission. He reached to the back of his belt and unclipped a thermal detonator. He set the detonator on a ten-second delay, placed it in the clone trooper's helmet, and then threw the helmet past the trees so it arced over the field and into the path of the approaching swoops.

Looking away from the swoops on his tail, Nuru turned his head just in time to see a white helmet tumble through the air in front of him.

Breaker?

He pushed hard at the swoop's maneuvering controls to avoid a collision with the helmet. As the helmet sailed past him, he saw a glint of metal inside it, and his instincts screamed *Grenade!*

The helmet bounced off the ground and was still rolling as Nuru pumped the brakes and spun the swoop through a tight turn that left him facing the incoming bikers. Letting go of the controls, he raised his hands and shouted, "Stop!"

The swoop gang didn't break or turn, but Nuru saw the giant's eyes go wide with surprise. And then the grenade detonated.

The shock wave tossed Nuru's swoop back through the air and nearly threw him from his saddle. The ground where the helmet had landed was now a gaping crater filled with a raging fireball that rapidly mushroomed into a tower of smoke. The shredded, blazing remains of swoops and bikers flew in all directions from the blast radius.

A wave of heat hit Nuru at the same time as the mangled remains of one human biker landed below his swoop. A split second later, the giant biker's body collapsed with a loud thud upon a slope that led up to a cluster of trees. Nuru had to fight back a feeling of nausea. He felt awful that his attempt to warn the bikers about the grenade had failed. Although the bikers had been hostile, he had never considered them enemies, and had never meant to lead them to their deaths.

But then, he had not been the one who had thrown the grenade. Looking beyond the body of the giant biker to the cluster of trees, he saw a shadowy figure climbing onto a speeder bike. Nuru gripped his swoop's controls, swung the swoop toward the trees, and rocketed forward.

As Nuru neared the trees, the mysterious biker

sped off into the forest. Nuru was about to give chase when he saw, out of the corner of his eye, a thrashing movement at the base of one tree. Turning his head, he found Breaker bound to the tree's trunk. Breaker was blindfolded and gagged, struggling to release himself. Although Nuru was immediately concerned and disturbed by the sight of Breaker so helpless, he was also relieved, for now he was certain that Breaker was not the man who had shot Sommilor and the others. He also felt guilty. *How could I have suspected Breaker?*

Nuru brought the swoop to a hovering stop near the fallen giant's body. He jumped off the swoop and ran to Breaker's side. "Breaker! Hold still!" He tugged off the blindfold and gag, then ignited his lightsaber and cut through the plastifiber bonds. In his haste, he failed to notice the leather utility belt that rested on the ground to his left.

"What hit me?" Breaker muttered, dazed. "Heard a loud bang and—" Breaker's eyes closed, and then his body went slack as he slid back into unconsciousness.

Nuru saw Breaker was still breathing. He switched on his comlink.

"Commander!" Sharp's voice came from the comm. "Are you all right? We saw the explosion from the spaceport and—!"

"I'm fine," Nuru interrupted, "but Breaker's down. Come get him." Leaving Breaker, he continued speaking as he ran back to the swoop. "The sniper fled into the woods. I can't let him escape."

"Sir, you should wait for us to—"

Nuru switched off the comlink and jumped back onto the swoop. He did not want to leave Breaker behind, but he could not risk losing the sniper. But just as he gripped the swoop's controls, the swoop jerked suddenly backward in the air, as if it had been snared by a powerful tractor beam.

Nuru glanced back and was stunned to see the orange-skinned giant standing upright, his arms wrapped around the back of the swoop. The giant's vest was smoldering, and a freshly blistered wound stretched across his left bicep. Nuru was about to reach for his lightsaber when the giant said, "That guy I saw taking off on a speeder bike. He a friend of yours?"

Still startled, Nuru shook his head. "He's a sniper," he said urgently. "He just shot some people.

I took the swoop to go after him."

"I got a bone to pick with him, too, so shove over!" The giant swung himself onto the swoop so he was seated behind Nuru, and the swoop shuddered under his weight. Before Nuru could protest, the giant reached past the boy's arms and seized the controls. The swoop's engine roared, and they launched into the woods.

Pressed back against the giant's chest, Nuru watched the trees whip past the swoop at a sickening speed. Raising his voice so he could be heard over the engine, he said, "I'm sorry about your friends."

"Those losers weren't my friends," the giant said as he tore through a small clearing. "I was just passing time."

"But . . . if they weren't your friends, why do you want to get the sniper?"

"He wasted my swoop!"

Nuru did not have to look at the speedometer to know they were traveling faster than he ever would have dared on his own through the densely wooded area. Although the giant steered the swoop with amazing agility, Nuru realized he was somewhat at the enormous biker's mercy.

Sharp had used his comlink to alert the other members of Breakout Squad that Nuru had gone after the sniper. Gunn and Chatterbox were already seated in the *Hasty Harpy*'s cockpit and had the engines up and running. Cleaver stood at the bottom of the *Harpy*'s boarding ramp at the spaceport, waiting for Sharp and Knuckles.

Against Cleaver's left thigh clung the magnetic gray-metal cylinder that he had found earlier on the ship's hull. The droid had hung on to the cylinder for the simple reason that Gunn had told him to save it for later, and his leg seemed like a practical place to keep it.

Cleaver saw Sharp and Knuckles running toward the *Harpy*. He said, "The Kynachi ship is secured?"

"Yes," Sharp answered as he hurried up the ramp with Knuckles and Cleaver right behind him. Leaving Knuckles and Cleaver in the main hold, Sharp grabbed his helmet and pulled it over his head before he ran to the cockpit.

The *Harpy* lifted off the ground, rotated

horizontally, then launched toward the column of smoke and fire that rose near the edge of the woods. Sharp arrived in the cockpit and saw Chatterbox was already wearing his own helmet. Gunn kept her eyes on the small inferno in front of her as she said, "Did the kid tell you how bad Breaker was hurt?"

"No," Sharp said. "Just that he was down."

Gunn guided the *Harpy* around the smoke and brought the ship close to the edge of the woods. Chatterbox leaned forward in his seat, pointed to the bottom of a tree, and said, "There's Breaker."

Gunn scowled. "Are you gonna talk all day or are you gonna go get him?" But Chatterbox was already following Sharp out of the cockpit.

Gunn adjusted the controls, and the *Harpy* came to a hover. Knuckles, Chatterbox, Sharp, and Cleaver were all carrying weapons as they spilled out of the ship. They ran to Breaker and found him still unconscious. They also found the leather utility belt that the sniper had left behind.

Cleaver snatched up the belt. The droid and Chatterbox watched for any sign of danger while Sharp and Knuckles lifted Breaker. When they were all back inside the *Harpy*'s main hold, Knuckles hit

the ship's intercom and said, "All on board, Gunn.
Let's find the commander."

Nuru struggled to remain calm as the giant
sent the swoop through the gap in a split-boughed
tree. Raising his voice so he could be heard over the
swoop's engine, Nuru shouted, "Did you see which
way the speeder went?"

"No."

"Then how do you know we're going the right
way?"

"Don't need to see him." The giant's nostrils
flared above the gold ring that dangled from his
nose. "I can smell his bike's exhaust trail."

Nuru saw shafts of light up ahead and realized
they were nearing the outer edge of the forest. The
giant bellowed, "What's your name, kid?"

"Nuru. What's yours?"

"Gizman. But call me Gizz. Everybody does."

With a loud rush of wind and swirling leaves,
the swoop burst out of the forest like a cumbersome
missile. A wide, grassy plain yawned out before

them, and beyond that, a rocky plateau.

Because Nuru had lost precious time while releasing Breaker from his bonds and making Gizz's acquaintance, he feared he had little chance of catching up with the sniper. But as the swoop tore over the grass, he sighted a distant object moving toward the plateau. It was the speeder bike. "There he is!"

"I'm on him."

Nuru locked his eyes on the speeder bike while Gizz accelerated, closing the distance between them and their quarry. They were still too far away for Nuru to have a clear view of the biker himself. Several seconds later, Gizz said, "Well, I'll be blasted."

"What's wrong?"

"He's heading for Shattered Rock."

"What's that?"

"Not what, where. Shattered Rock's a canyon."

"Is it hazardous?"

Gizz grinned. "That's one way of putting it." He twisted the throttle, and the swoop rocketed after the fleeing bike.

CHAPTER 9

Hudu Shiv knew the Jedi might try to pursue him. But as he rode his speeder back to the canyon where he had left his starship, he was surprised when he glanced back and saw the swoop coming up fast on his tail. He was further surprised to see his pursuer was not Nuru Kungurama, but the largest member of the swoop gang that he had bombed and left for dead. But then he noticed the small, blue-skinned boy seated in front of the giant biker, and he was even more surprised. Not only had the giant survived the blast, but he was apparently allied with the Jedi, if only for the moment.

Shiv calculated that the more powerful swoop

would overtake him in seconds. He popped open a control panel that was built into the left handlebar and pressed a button.

Nuru and Gizz were less than thirty meters behind the speeder bike and gaining fast when they both saw more than a dozen small objects eject from behind the biker's saddle. As the objects fell away from the bike and bounced across the hard ground, Gizz muttered, "Aw, poodoo."

The objects were compact concussion grenades. Nuru doubted that Gizz would be able to swerve around the explosives, not at their present speed. Without warning, Gizz jerked the controls and launched the swoop into a steep ascent just as the nearest grenades detonated. Nuru squinted his eyes as he found himself unexpectedly facing Vaced's sun, and then a blast of hot dust caught the swoop's tail, jouncing the riders as they continued to race for the sky. The remaining grenades detonated in a rippling series of explosions beneath them.

Gizz struggled with the swoop's controls, briefly

leveling off before he steered into a dive. Nuru saw they were descending straight at the speeder bike, which flew like a dart, close to its own shadow, dangerously low over the ground, heading for the mouth of a ravine. Gizz held his course behind the sniper but stayed well above the ground to avoid traveling into the path of more grenades.

They followed the speeder bike into the ravine. Nuru had never before seen anything quite like the vibrantly colorful rock formations that lined the walls, but thanks to his education at the Jedi Temple, he recognized them as petrified trees. Most were columnar formations, but some ancient boughs and limbs had transformed into strangely twisted, sharp-edged coils of intertwined stone.

Nuru saw the swoop's shadow snaking along the rocky wall to his left. As they followed the biker through a bend in the ravine, the shadow began gliding rapidly downward over the rocks, and Nuru realized it was about to slide into the sniper's visual range. Not wanting to alert the sniper to the swoop's position, Nuru was about to caution Gizz when he noticed Gizz had just removed one hand from the swoop's controls so he could draw his blaster pistol.

Gizz fired at the same moment that the swoop's shadow slid across the ravine floor, right in front of the speeder bike.

Evidently, the sniper saw the shadow because he swerved slightly for no other apparent reason. As the fired energy bolt sailed past his shoulder and slammed into the ground, the sniper held tight to the controls with one hand while yanking his blaster rifle free from its sling, then swiftly tilted the weapon back so its long barrel rested against his shoulder. Without glancing back, he squeezed the trigger, launching an energy bolt straight at Nuru and Gizz.

Nuru saw the incoming bolt and calculated that it would strike Gizz's upper body. Because Gizz only had one hand on the swoop's controls, Nuru had just enough elbow room to draw and ignite his lightsaber. He extended the blade forward at a sharp angle, and the fired bolt smacked into the blade and rebounded into the ravine wall.

"Don't kill him, Gizz!" Nuru said. "I need to question him!"

"Son of a nerf herder!" Gizz roared at the sight of the lightsaber. Still holding his blaster, he said, "You're a Jedi?"

"Look out!" Nuru cried as he deactivated his blade and pushed against Gizz's left wrist. The swoop tilted hard to the left just in time to avoid striking a broad overhanging limb of a petrified tree.

"You got nothing on me!" Gizz said as he holstered his blaster. Returning both hands to the control bars, he continued, "I wasn't anywhere near the Zygian Savings and Loan on Treylon II three months ago!"

"I don't know what you're talking about. We're both after the sniper, remember?"

"Oh. Right. The sniper."

As Gizz steered around a bend and the swoop hurtled past more stony limbs, Nuru said, "I've lost him."

"My nose hasn't." Gizz lifted a thick finger away from a handlebar and pointed downward. "Look there."

Nuru followed Gizz's gaze and saw the sniper racing across the bottom of the ravine, deftly steering his speeder past a cluster of immense boulders. The sniper zipped into a dark chasm. Nuru said, "Where does that gap lead?"

"Nowhere!" Gizz snorted. "We've got him

trapped!" He kicked the foot pedals and descended after the speeder bike. Nuru felt his stomach clench as Gizz took a steep shortcut through a tangle of rock formations before he leveled off fast, barely three meters off the ground.

They were zooming toward the chasm when Nuru sensed danger, and then a sudden pang of dread. A moment later, the sniper launched out of the chasm, heading straight for the swoop, with his rifle held forward. Nuru was still registering the fact that the sniper must have circled back within the chasm when the sniper fired.

Gizz was hunched forward on the swoop. Both hands gripping the control bars, his body practically wrapped around Nuru, leaving the Jedi unable to draw his lightsaber without harming the monstrous biker. All Nuru could do was duck as the energy bolt smashed into Gizz's upper chest. Gizz howled in pain and rage. The sniper fired again, and the swoop's control vanes exploded into metal shreds.

And then Nuru had a clear view of the figure on the speeder bike. He was startled that the figure was clad in the unmistakable armor of a Mandalorian warrior.

The damaged swoop plunged toward the ravine's floor. Nuru was confident that he could leap away safely, but was less certain that he could do anything to help Gizz. Before Nuru could do anything, he was caught in the crook of Gizz's left arm, and then the giant tumbled off the swoop, taking Nuru with him.

The swoop hit the ground and exploded at the same moment that Gizz's body struck the ground with an ugly thud and rolled across hard rock, his arms wrapped protectively around Nuru. They rolled over a wide patch of dead weeds and didn't stop rolling until Gizz smacked into the base of an enormous, multicolored boulder.

Hudu Shiv raced past the boulder where the young Jedi lay motionless with the swoop biker. He glanced back, and then brought his bike to a shuddering stop. Count Dooku had instructed Shiv not to reveal his Mandalorian identity to the Jedi or clone troopers on Vaced, and Shiv silently cursed himself for having entered a chasm with only one exit. He was certain that the Jedi had gotten a good look at his armor, but he did not know whether the boy had survived the fall from the swoop. Shiv knew what to do next. He gunned the bike's engine and turned around, heading back toward the boulder.

Nuru opened his eyes and saw the sky directly above him. He was lying on his back across Gizz's chest, pinned under the heavy weight of Gizz's right arm. He groaned, although Gizz had absorbed most of the impact when they hit the ground. But he could hardly blame Gizz for pulling him off the swoop, for it seemed Gizz had only been trying to prevent Nuru from dying in a fiery crash.

"Gizz? Can you hear me?" Gizz did not respond, but Nuru felt the giant's chest swell slightly. He was still breathing.

Nuru heard the sniper's speeder bike grow louder as it approached. The bike's whining engine sounded as if it were on the other side of the boulder, and Nuru imagined the sniper was circling back. He shoved at Gizz's arm and rolled off the giant. Snatching his lightsaber from his belt, he activated its blade as he stepped through the long-dead weeds, moving away from Gizz, and then waited for the speeder bike to appear from around the boulder.

As expected, the speeder bike glided into view. However, Nuru was surprised to see the bike's saddle was empty. The bike was automatically slowing to a stop when Nuru sensed something move behind him. Nuru realized the sniper had used the bike as a decoy. He turned fast and saw the sniper standing only four meters away, his rifle leveled at Nuru.

The sniper fired, but Nuru had already leaped high into the air. As Nuru executed a flip that briefly planted his feet against the boulder, he noted that it was not an energy bolt that left the sniper's rifle but a slender projectile, possibly a dart. Holding his lightsaber in his right hand so its blade was tucked dangerously close to the side of his body, he kicked off from the boulder, flipped again, and landed on his feet directly behind the sniper.

Hudu Shiv had studied holorecordings of Jedi in action and was not surprised by Kungurama's speed or acrobatic ability. Still, he regretted that he had not been able to fell Kungurama with a tranquilizer dart. Without turning to face the boy, he shifted his grip on his rifle as he repositioned his feet, bracing himself before he made a sudden jabbing motion that sent his rifle's butt straight into Nuru's sternum.

Nuru stumbled back but managed to swing his blade up through the butt and trigger mechanism of the sniper's rifle. The sniper threw the damaged rifle at Nuru. Nuru dodged the rifle and was about to leap forward when the sniper extended one fist and activated the flamethrower built into his gauntlet.

The blast of flame struck the ground in front of Nuru. Nuru leaped again, somersaulting in the air to land beside the sniper. Holding his lightsaber away from his body, he slapped his free hand down on the sniper's gauntlet, forcing the jet of flames away from both of them. But then the sniper rotated his arm, deactivating the flamethrower as he grabbed Nuru's right wrist. The sniper twisted hard, forcing Nuru's hand back and causing the Jedi's fingers to lose their grip on his lightsaber. The lightsaber's blade flickered out as it fell to the ground. The sniper kept his grip locked on Nuru's wrist as he brought one knee up into the boy's stomach.

Nuru felt the wind get knocked out of him. He blocked the pain from his mind and reached fast with his left hand to his belt. His fingers wrapped around Ring Sol-Ambase's lightsaber. The sniper was about to kick him again when Nuru thumbed the lightsaber's activation switch and the blade blazed to life.

All Nuru had to do was flick his wrist and the sniper would be cut in half. But he wanted to subdue the sniper and question him, not kill him. He took a fraction of a second to readjust his grip on Ambase's lightsaber as he prepared to deliver a strike that would only injure the man, but that fraction was enough for him to lose his advantage.

The sniper shoved Nuru away from him. The lightsaber's blade flashed past the sniper's chest as Nuru stumbled back. The sniper's hands flew to his belt, and he drew both blaster pistols. Nuru recovered his footing and kept Ambase's lightsaber in front of him, waiting for the sniper to open fire.

They both heard the sound of an approaching starship. Nuru recognized the familiar sound of the *Hasty Harpy*'s engines. He was not surprised that Breakout Squad had been able to locate him so fast as the rising flames and smoke from the ruined swoop must have drawn their attention.

Keeping his gaze on the armored man and Ambase's lightsaber extended, Nuru reached out with the Force to make his own lightsaber fly up from the ground and land in his waiting palm. He activated his lightsaber so its blade blazed beside the other. He had little doubt that he could deflect blaster bolts faster than the man could squeeze his triggers. He said, "Surrender at once."

He did not expect the sniper to fire low, launching a stream of energy bolts that hammered at the rocky ground in front of Nuru's feet. The blasts kicked stones and sand up into the air, spraying dust into his eyes, and he reflexively squeezed his eyes shut. Fortunately, he remained alert, using the Force to guide his actions and anticipate the next attack.

But it did not come. Instead, the armored man ran for his speeder bike.

Eyes still closed, Nuru sensed the sniper's departure and ran blindly after him, relying on the Force to maintain his course and allow him to visualize the terrain, his opponent, and the bike. Because he had already learned the hard way that the sniper was an incredibly skilled up-close fighter, he chose not to tackle him. He leaped high into the air, holding both lightsabers out and away from his body, and somersaulted over the sniper, angling himself to land beside the bike. As he descended, both lightsabers swept through the bike's maneuvering fins and central repulsor pod, crippling the vehicle. He landed on his feet at the same moment that the ruined speeder crashed to the ground, and then he opened his eyes, which still stung from the sand.

The sniper took a quick sidestep and darted out of sight around the boulder that loomed beside Gizz, whose unconscious form still rested amid the weeds. Nuru heard the *Harpy*'s landing jets. The freighter touched down close enough for him to see Gunn and Chatterbox in the cockpit.

Brandishing blaster rifles, Knuckles, Sharp, and Cleaver rushed out of the *Harpy* and ran over to Nuru. Knuckles said, "We got Breaker. Are you all right, Commander?"

Nuru responded with a single nod, although the truth was he felt battered and bruised. "The sniper ran behind that boulder," he said as he switched off Ambase's lightsaber and returned it to his belt. "Did you see him? He's wearing Mandalorian armor."

"Mandalorian?" Knuckles said with disbelief. Like most Republic troopers, he was aware of the warrior culture that had lasted thousands of years in the Mandalore sector. He also knew that Jango Fett himself had been a Mandalorian and that Fett's own armor had served as the basis for the armor worn by Knuckles and his comrades. "But Mandalore is a peaceful world now," Knuckles continued. "Maybe he's a renegade or an impostor."

Sharp said, "Or maybe a former Mandalorian warrior, like Jango Fett."

"Whoever he is, he knows how to fight," Nuru said. "What's the condition of Sommilor and his men? And who's watching them?"

Knuckles and Sharp looked at Nuru through their visors. Knuckles said, "Sorry, Commander. We thought you knew. Sommilor and the pilots are dead."

Nuru was stunned. "What?"

"The toxic darts that hit them were lethal. We secured their bodies inside their ship. We didn't—"

Knuckles was interrupted by a loud roar that came from behind the boulder. A spray of burning fuel launched out across the dead weeds that blanketed the ground. Nuru realized the sniper had activated his flamethrower again, and as the weeds caught fire, he saw the flames licking toward Gizz's body. He pointed at Gizz and said, "Get him out of there!"

Without questioning the command, Knuckles, Sharp, and Cleaver jumped through the rising flames while Nuru kept his eyes peeled for the sniper. The two troopers and the droid grabbed the giant and dragged him away from the boulder as fast as they could, stomping at the flames as they went. The fire was still spreading as they neared the *Harpy*.

Nuru was backing away from the fire, saw that it was still spreading, and said, "Get him into the ship."

Knuckles said, "Commander, are you sure we should—?"

"He saved my life!"

The troopers and the droid hauled Gizz up the *Harpy*'s boarding ramp and were struggling to maneuver him through the hatch when Nuru saw the sniper emerge at the other side of the boulder, moving past the remains of the speeder bike. The sniper was still gripping both of his blaster pistols.

Nuru raised his left hand and used the Force to push the sniper off his feet. The sniper was flung sideways through the air and might have crashed against the ravine wall except he fired his jetpack and launched skyward, rapidly rising higher than

Nuru could jump. Nuru held his lightsaber steadily as the sniper ascended, ready to defend himself if his opponent opened fire.

Shiv grimaced behind his helmet as he lifted away from the Jedi. He had only intended to find out whether the boy was still alive and shoot a tranquilizer dart to subdue him if necessary, but not to engage him in combat. He imagined Dooku would be furious, but that was not Shiv's immediate concern. He could not permit anyone to claim and analyze the Death Watch arsenal on his abandoned bike.

As he continued to rise, he reached to his belt and tapped a button, triggering a remote detonator. Down below, the remains of his bike exploded into fire and dust, and the power of the blast sent the Jedi sprawling. Seeing the Jedi tumble away from the explosion, Shiv realized he was disappointed by his first encounter with a Jedi. He wondered whether he would ever get a chance to duel with one who was mature.

Shiv scanned the terrain for his *Pursuer*-class

enforcement ship and found it right where he had landed it. He flew straight toward the ship.

The fleeing sniper had just moved out of sight as Nuru pushed himself up off the ground. The air was now heavy with smoke. A moment later, he felt hands grab his upper arms, and he was yanked to his feet. Slightly dazed, he realized Knuckles and Sharp had come back for him.

As the clones rushed him back to the *Harpy*, Nuru gasped, "Have to stop him." They were no sooner up the boarding ramp when the *Harpy* lifted off and shot up and out of the ravine.

Nuru, Knuckles, and Sharp stumbled into the main hold. They found Cleaver busily strapping Gizz's body to the deck beside Breaker, who was strapped to a bunk. Both Gizz and Breaker remained unconscious. Cleaver looked up at Nuru and said, "I had to secure this man to the deck because the *Harpy* isn't equipped with a bunk large enough for him."

Nuru was so focused on apprehending the sniper that he barely heard the droid. He left the hold and moved fast to the cockpit. Stepping up behind Gunn and Chatterbox, he crouched down between their seats so he had a better view through the window in front of them. He saw the sniper still airborne, less than thirty meters in front of the *Harpy*.

"That jetpack can't carry him far," Nuru said. "He'll have to land soon."

"I could bring him down right now if you want," Gunn said as she gestured to the controls for the laser cannons.

"No! I want him alive for questioning."

Gunn sighed. "Have it your way."

Nuru leaned forward to get a wider view of the land below. He spotted an angular transport that rested beside the base of a cliff in the canyon. He recognized the model as a *Pursuer*-class enforcement ship, used by Mandalorians as a patrol and transport vessel, but also popular with various police forces and bounty hunters throughout the galaxy. He said, "There's a ship down there. He must be heading—"

Nuru was surprised yet again by a sudden feeling of imminent danger. Before he could warn Gunn to take evasive action, the flying man executed a midair twist, faced the *Harpy*, and bent at the waist.

Nuru shouted, "No!"

But the man clad in Mandalorian armor had already launched the missile from his jetpack.

CHAPTER 10

The explosion was tremendous. The Z-6 antivehicle homing missile had struck and detonated with a thunderous boom against the *Hasty Harpy*'s lower hull. Lalo Gunn screamed as if her own body had taken the hit directly, while Chatterbox clung to the controls in front of him. Nuru, who had not been belted into a seat, was thrown off his feet and bounced off the cockpit's low ceiling.

Another explosion rocked the *Harpy*. Nuru gripped the back of Chatterbox's seat and pulled himself up off the deck. Through the cockpit's window, he saw they were plunging rapidly toward the canyon called Shattered Rock.

Chatterbox said, "We're losing altitude."

Desperately pushing switches and levers as she checked a status readout, Gunn replied, "Tell me something I don't know already!"

"We lost all shields, landing jets, and the primary port thruster."

"I know that, too, so just shut up!" Gunn wrestled with the controls to stabilize the ship. An awful mechanical groan rumbled through the *Harpy* as Gunn somehow brought the nose up.

Through the window, Nuru was relieved to see they were no longer falling toward Vaced, but the ship was still listing hard to the left. "You have to bring us down, Gunn. I can't let the assassin get away."

"Maybe you didn't hear, kid, but *he blew away our landing jets*! I'm gonna have to make an emergency landing, and I'm betting it will hurt. You should have let me blast him when I had the chance!"

Nuru knew that Gunn's ship was equipped with escape pods. He was about to suggest that they evacuate when he remembered Gizz back in the main hold. Gizz could barely fit through the *Harpy*'s main hatch, let alone any of the escape pods.

"You can bring us down safely, Gunn," Nuru said. "I know you can."

"I can't tell you how much that means to me," Gunn said sarcastically.

Nuru frowned. It was bad enough that he had failed to protect Sommilor and the two Kynachi pilots, but now he had endangered everyone on the *Harpy*, too. He suddenly felt an almost overwhelming sense of failure.

And yet, he still wanted to go after the assassin. He knew he had made a terrible mistake in underestimating the man's fighting ability, but now he wondered if he had also erred in trying to capture the man alive.

Should I have tried to kill him?

Deep within himself, Nuru felt something stir, a strange sensation that was neither warm nor cold but . . . dark.

The *Harpy* wobbled as it tore across the sky, trailing fire and smoke.

Hudu Shiv glanced back at the disabled freighter

as his jetpack carried him down to Vaced's surface. If the Jedi and other passengers on the freighter considered themselves lucky to be still alive, Shiv would take credit for that. After all, he had aimed his missile at the lower hull, not at the cockpit or anywhere near the fuel tanks.

He descended close to his *Pursuer*, killed the jetpack, and hit the ground running. He used a remote to deactivate the ship's security system, entered the ship fast, and grabbed some equipment. He knew if Nuru Kungurama survived, the boy would alert his superiors about seeing a man wearing Mandalorian armor on Vaced. Shiv would do what was necessary to discourage the Jedi from ever hunting him down.

The *Hasty Harpy* was listing hard but still airborne. In the cockpit, Nuru had belted himself into a seat behind Gunn and Chatterbox. Over the intercom, they heard Knuckles say, "We've got a fire in the aft hold, Captain."

"Then put it out!" Gunn snapped. She glanced at one of the few scopes that was still working. "The terrain-following sensor is blown, but I still got eyes. I'll bring her down in the field between the spaceport and the woods." She tilted her chin back toward the intercom. "Listen up, everyone! It's too late for fire fighting! Buckle up now because we're gonna—"

A hail of laserfire streaked past the cockpit, and then a stream of energy bolts smashed into the *Harpy*'s upper hull, startling everyone in the cockpit. "Stang!" Gunn cursed as the *Harpy* buckled at the impact. "Who's shooting at us *now*?!"

A moment later, the attacking ship zoomed over the *Harpy* and swung into view. It was the *Pursuer*-class ship that Nuru had seen earlier. He had no doubt that the armored assassin was piloting the craft, and that his goal was to bring down the *Harpy*.

"That tears it," Gunn snarled as she shoved the controls, sending the *Harpy* into a sudden roll that caused the engines to howl. The *Harpy* belched black smoke as she emerged from the roll and lifted up behind the *Pursuer*. Nuru saw Gunn reach to a red switch on the weapons console. He did not try to stop her from pressing it.

The *Harpy*'s missile launchers fired. Two homing missiles zinged toward the *Pursuer*, which banked suddenly to the left. The missiles raced after the targeted ship, then arced out slightly before they accelerated, each angling for a different side of the *Pursuer*. The missiles slammed into the ship and detonated. The *Pursuer* erupted in a bright burst that sent blazing debris across the sky over Shattered Rock.

Gunn let out a whistle. "That felt pretty good," she said as she banked back toward the spaceport. "Now comes the rough part."

Gunn punched the accelerator and pressed a switch, and the *Harpy* lurched up. An alarm began wailing, Nuru could not tell whether it came from the spaceport or the cockpit. The *Harpy* wobbled as she glided over the landing pads, banked hard as she crossed over the adjoining field, and then dropped.

The *Harpy* skidded across the ground, crushing the high grasses and leaving a rough trench in her wake. She shuddered violently and came to a stop, just as the firefighter droids arrived from the spaceport.

"End of the road," Gunn said dismally.

Nuru released his safety belt. "I'm going to check on the others." He went back to the main hold, where he found Sharp and Knuckles already working to release the unconscious Gizz from the floor. Breaker's eyes were open, and Cleaver was helping him up from the bunk. Breaker shook his head and said, "Did I miss something?"

"We'll fill you in after we're all outside," Nuru said, gesturing to the main hatch. But as he turned, he noticed a leather utility belt lying on the deck. He picked up the belt and looked at it with astonishment. "Where did this come from?"

"I found it near Breaker in the woods," Cleaver said. "I'm sorry I neglected to mention it, but we were a bit rushed. I suspect it belonged to the sniper."

Nuru continued staring at the belt for a moment, then reached to his own belt and removed Ring Sol-Ambase's lightsaber. He secured the lightsaber to a clip on the belt that Cleaver had recovered. "No, Cleaver. This didn't belong to the sniper."

The belt had three attached pouches. Two were empty. One was not.

"What the skrag hit me?" Gizz moaned as he sat up on the ground a few meters from the wreckage of the *Hasty Harpy*, where Cleaver was helping the firefighting droids extinguish the small fires that were still burning.

"Take it easy, Gizz," Nuru said. "You might have a concussion."

Gizz looked at Nuru, and then noticed the four clone troopers who stood nearby, listening to an official from the spaceport. The troopers had removed their helmets. Gizz blinked his eyes and scowled. "Something's wrong with my vision. I'm seeing quadruple."

Nuru grinned. "They're clones."

"Oh," Gizz said. "Hey, what happened to that armored guy we went after, the one who blasted my swoop?"

Nuru nodded. "He's dead."

"This day's just getting better." Gizz yawned. "I got a whopping headache. I'm gonna rest my eyes a bit." He lay back on the ground and began snoring almost immediately.

Nuru looked over to the spaceport official, who was a stern-looking man. The man said, "I should have known Gizz was involved in this crash. Ever since he arrived on Vaced, he's been trouble. And no one's going to mourn that gang he hung out with."

Nuru shook his head. "Gizz isn't responsible for what happened here."

"Well, I got plenty of other reasons to send him to prison! Disturbing the peace, public insobriety, failure to pay debts ..." Glancing at Gizz's slumbering form, he continued, "I'm going to see to it that Gizz goes straight to some off-world prison, maybe the Spice Mines of Kessel. Keep an eye on him while I get some chains." He turned and headed for one of the buildings at the spaceport.

When the man was out of earshot, Nuru said, "We're leaving. Now."

"You got a weird sense of humor, kid," Gunn said.

"I'm serious. We'll take Sommilor's ship. We'll take the bodies of Sommilor and his pilots with us."

"Back to Coruscant?" Sharp said.

"Not immediately." Nuru held out the utility belt. "This is Master Ambase's. Cleaver found it in the woods near Breaker. The assassin must have dropped it. And I found *this* in one of the utility pouches." He reached into a pocket and pulled out a small disc-shaped device. It was an imagecaster, a compact hologram projector. He activated the imagecaster, and a holographic readout materialized above the disc. The readout was a three-dimensional map of the Bilbringi system, complete with navigational coordinates. "Bilbringi Depot isn't far from here. Maybe the assassin brought my Master to Bilbringi and left him there. I need to find out."

"Begging your pardon, Commander," Sharp said, "but shouldn't we contact the authorities on Coruscant first and let them know what happened to Sommilor and his pilots?"

"No," Nuru said sharply. "No transmissions to Coruscant. Someone has been tracking us across space, possibly manipulating our movements. We never did find the transmitter on the *Harpy*, but I'm not taking any more chances. We'll contact the authorities *after* we investigate Bilbringi."

"You're crazy, kid," Gunn said. "How do you know the assassin didn't leave that belt behind on purpose? Maybe he was trying to lure you and the rest of us into a trap on Bilbringi!"

"I considered that possibility," Nuru admitted as he deactivated the imagecaster. "But the fact that the assassin attacked the *Harpy* suggests otherwise. I don't believe he was trying to lead us anywhere. He was trying to kill us. We may never know who he was or what his motives were, but we know he won't harm anyone again."

"Well, count me out, anyway," Gunn said. "You helped get me off of Kynachi, and in return, I took you to Chiss space and back. But if I'd known I'd be making a detour to a black hole, tangling with space pirates, chasing a killer wearing a missile on his back, and that the *Harpy* would wind up like *this* . . ." She gestured to her ruined ship and shook her head. "Forget it. I'll find some other way off Vaced. I'm through traveling with you."

Nuru sighed. "I'm sorry about the *Harpy*. I promise, when I return to Coruscant, I will submit a request to the Jedi Council to have the Republic reimburse you for—"

"You're assuming you'll *ever* return to Coruscant," Gunn interrupted. "What good is your promise if you go to Bilbringi and you get yourself and everyone else killed?!"

"That's enough, Lalo," Chatterbox said.

Everyone looked at Chatterbox. He had never addressed Gunn by her first name before.

"Sorry, Nuru," Gunn said quietly. "I trust your promise is good." Then she stepped up close to Chatterbox, looked him straight in the eye, and said, "I'd ask you to stay with me, but I already know your answer. So long, Chatterbox." She turned and started to move away.

Chatterbox grabbed Gunn's arm and pulled her back to him. He kissed her. She kissed him back.

Knuckles checked his rifle. Breaker looked up at the sky. Sharp lowered his head and stared at his boots. Nuru fidgeted with the imagecaster. Cleaver walked over from the wreckage and said, "The fires are all out."

"Not from where I'm standing," Gunn said as she drew away from Chatterbox. She reached up, tapped his lips, and said, "Be careful with that mouth of yours." She glanced at the other members of Breakout Squad and said, "Bye, boys."

Sharp said, "Where will you go?"

"I might just call an old friend to give me a lift." Then Gunn walked off toward the spaceport with her head held high. She did not look back.

Knuckles looked at the sleeping giant and said, "Do we just leave him there?"

"He may have a criminal record," Nuru said, "but he *did* save me from a nasty crash. I imagine he might be quite grateful if he doesn't wake up in prison."

Sharp said, "You're not suggesting we take him with us?"

Nuru nodded. "I'm trusting my instincts, Sharp. I suspect Gizz hasn't had an easy life. I believe he deserves another chance." He looked at Chatterbox and said, "You spent a lot of hours in the *Harpy*'s cockpit. Think you can fly Sommilor's freighter?"

Chatterbox nodded.

"Good. Now, let's get going before that spaceport guy comes back."

As they hauled Gizz to Sommilor's freighter, no one noticed the small, gray magnetic cylinder that was still attached to Cleaver's left leg.

Almost half an hour after the *Hasty Harpy* crashed in the grassy field on Vaced, the Suwantek Systems freighter lifted off, carrying a young Jedi, four Republic troopers, a refurbished droid commando, a giant named Gizz, and the bodies of three dead men from Kynachi. As the freighter ascended from Vaced Spaceport, a lone man, standing on a plateau at Shattered Rock, watched the departure through his macrobinoculars.

Hudu Shiv lowered the macrobinoculars. Satisfied that the Jedi and his allies had left the planet, he walked over to the emergency lifeboat that rested nearby. He had disengaged the lifeboat from his *Pursuer* just before he had used a remote control transmitter to send the *Pursuer* after Kungurama's ship. And then, after using the remote to fire a few blasts at Kungurama's ship, he had allowed the *Pursuer* to be destroyed.

Shiv imagined Count Dooku would express displeasure when he learned Nuru Kungurama had sighted a Mandalorian warrior on Vaced. However, Shiv had covered his trail by faking his own death and had also accomplished his primary goals. The men from Kynachi were dead, and a Jedi utility belt had been left at the shooting site.

Shiv climbed into the lifeboat. He had already plotted a course for a nearby space station where he would be picked up by a covert Death Watch transport. He punched the ignition, and the lifeboat launched from the plateau, leaving a trail of water vapor as it raced up through the atmosphere.

He wondered if he might cross paths with Nuru Kungurama again. As much as Shiv prided himself for being a professional, he could not deny he wanted another crack at the Jedi who had failed to kill him.

CHAPTER 11

"You got any more food on this ship?" the giant, Gizz, asked.

"No, Gizz," Nuru said. "You ate it all."

"Oh." Gizz scratched his stomach. "The station you said we're going to . . ."

"Bilbringi Depot."

"Yeah, Bilbringi. We can get more food there, right?" Gizz added.

"I hope so."

They were sitting on a bench beside a console in the cargo bay of the Suwantek Systems freighter. Nuru had directed the troopers to place Gizz in the cargo bay because the passenger compartments did not have sufficient headroom for the giant. The bodies of Sommilor and the two pilots had been neatly bagged and carefully stowed in the bay's airtight storage chamber. A nearby window offered a view of hyperspace as they raced to their destination.

Nuru looked at a chronometer on the nav console and said, "We'll be exiting hyperspace soon."

"Thanks for not leaving me on Vaced. I overheard the clones talking. They said that I might have woken up in chains or in prison. You didn't have to bring me with you."

"You didn't have to pull me off that swoop before it crashed at Shattered Rock."

Gizz shrugged. "Don't give me too much credit. I was probably just saving myself at the time and took you with me." He looked at the window. "I've never been to Bilbringi Depot, but I've heard about it. It's on an asteroid owned by a Hutt named Drixo. Tell me again, why are we going there?"

"I'm searching for my Jedi Master. I have reason to believe he may have been taken to Bilbringi, and—"

"Excuse me, Commander," Breaker interrupted as he entered the cargo bay. "We may have a situation." He walked over to the nav console and pressed a series of buttons. "See here."

Nuru got up from the bench and examined the console's data display. "What's this? Frequency readouts?"

"Wait."

And then Nuru saw a tiny green circle flash on the display. Nuru's eyes went wide. Calming himself, he said, "So . . . Sommilor's ship is carrying a hidden transmitter. You just discovered this?"

Breaker nodded. "Commander, we don't know what to expect at Bilbringi Depot, but thanks to that transmitter, it's entirely possible that someone at Bilbringi is expecting *us*."

Gizz lifted his girth off the bench and said, "I got news for you, clone. No one at Bilbringi is expecting *me*." He placed a massive hand on Nuru's shoulder. "If anyone's messing with my little buddy here, they're in for a galaxy of pain."

"In that case," Breaker said, "I guess we have nothing to worry about."

The freighter dropped out of hyperspace in the Bilbringi system. Nuru had joined Chatterbox in the cockpit, and he watched as the freighter moved past countless asteroids toward the largest one, designated Bilbringi VII, the home of Bilbringi Depot.

Nuru had informed the other members of Breakout Squad about the transmission signal that Breaker had discovered. "Easy does it, Chatterbox," Nuru said as they neared Bilbringi VII. "We don't know for a fact whether some enemy is waiting for us. For all we know, we may appear on their scopes as an ordinary freighter."

Soon, they were able to make out details of the depot through the cockpit window. Bright lights illuminated a cluster of landing pads, modular structures, and docking bays. And then Nuru spotted the barges and a large Metalorn yacht.

Nuru gasped. "That's Overseer Umbrag's ship." He hit the intercom. "Umbrag's at Bilbringi Depot. No Separatist warships in sight, just some drone barges and Umbrag's yacht. Knuckles and Sharp, are the laser cannons primed?"

"Yes, Commander," Knuckles responded.

"Breaker?"

"I'm all set with Cleaver and Gizz, Commander."

"We're about to dock," Nuru said. "Be ready for anything."

Gizz added, "I don't even know who Umbrag is, but I'm itching to clobber him."

Overseer Umbrag was lounging in Drixo the Hutt's former lair, playing a starfighter hologame, when he heard a clamor from the outer corridor.

A moment later, he heard the clattering approach of a battle droid. The droid said, "A Suwantek Systems freighter just arrived, sir."

Without looking up from his game, Umbrag said, "Tell them the same thing you said to the other ships that tried to dock after us. Tell them the depot is under quarantine."

"I tried telling them, sir. But they didn't listen. They just blasted me."

"What?" Umbrag looked at the droid through his thick goggles and was startled to see both of its arms had been blown off. "This is an outrage! Who dared to defy my order?!"

"Well, there were a few Republic troopers, a very angry giant, a young Jedi, and a droid commando who doesn't seem to be on our side anymore."

"A Jedi?" Umbrag said nervously. "Did he have blue skin and red eyes?"

A voice bellowed from behind the dismembered droid, "You must be Umbrag." Umbrag looked past the droid, saw an orange-skinned humanoid monster standing beside Nuru Kungurama, and fainted.

"That battle went much more easily than I imagined it would," Cleaver said.

"No kidding," Knuckles added. "If you ask me, it was *too* easy. I'm just disappointed we couldn't find any evidence that General Ambase was ever here."

"The fight might not be over yet," Breaker said as he tossed a battle droid's head into a pile of droid parts they had collected on Bilbringi Depot. "We blasted eleven droids, but they may have arrived here as an even dozen."

"If there's a straggler, we'll get him, too," Sharp said confidently. He gestured to the pile of vanquished droids. "It doesn't make sense. Why would the Separatists take over Bilbringi Depot, then leave only a few battle droids to defend it?"

Chatterbox responded with a shrug. Breaker said, "Maybe Umbrag will tell us when he regains consciousness."

Breakout Squad was standing in the Bilbringi Depot docking bay next to their appropriated freighter. The troopers had removed their helmets. Gizz walked past them, carrying Umbrag over one shoulder as he headed for the freighter's boarding ramp. Nuru stood at the base of the ramp and said, "Thanks, Gizz. You can put him in the hold for now."

"Gladly," Gizz replied as he carried Umbrag into the ship.

Nuru walked over to the troopers and Cleaver. "I transmitted a message to the Jedi Council. I told them what happened on Vaced and also here at the depot. A Republic cruiser should arrive here shortly to transport us back to Coruscant."

Knuckles said, "What about Sommilor's ship?"

"It will likely be taken to Kynachi, so the men's bodies can be returned to their families." Nuru shook his head. "Those men had counted on me to escort them to Coruscant. I'll never forget my failure on Vaced."

A silence fell over the group. Gizz stepped out of the freighter, walked past the others, and said, "I'm gonna look for some food."

As Gizz headed out of the docking bay, Cleaver looked at Nuru and said, "It wasn't your fault, Commander. You didn't kill those men. The assassin did. A Jedi can't save everyone all the time."

"Cleaver's right, Commander," Breaker said. "What's more, none of us might have survived Kynachi if it weren't for you."

"And consider what we *did* accomplish," Knuckles added. "We finally nabbed Umbrag! And judging from the cargo in his drone barges, it looks like we may have stopped the Separatists from transforming the depot into some kind of manufacturing facility."

Sharp said, "With any luck, we'll also get information out of Umbrag that will help us find General Ambase."

Nuru frowned. Breaker said, "What's wrong, Commander?"

"Something just occurred to me. When we return to Coruscant, I doubt the Council will encourage me to continue serving with Breakout Squad. I'm sure they'll assign you to a more experienced leader. I just want you all to know I've learned a great deal from you, and . . . and I'll miss you all very much."

"Commander," Breaker said, "I think I can speak for all the men, and Cleaver, too, when I say it's been an honor to serve with—"

Breaker was interrupted by the sound of a starship approaching the docking bay. Turning to see the incoming ship, Nuru was amazed to see a teardrop-shaped transport with a recessed cockpit ⸻ a single sharp-tipped maneuvering fin. The ship ⸻ ⸻ed in a luminescent energy field that ⸻ ⸻ie, pale white light. As the transport ⸻ ⸻ard the docking bay, Knuckles ⸻ a ship like that before."

⸻ I," Nuru said. "Put on your ⸻ weapons, and take cover." The ⸻ obeyed, moving quickly behind ⸻ containers.

⸻ p slid into the docking bay. No ⸻ led as it came to a hovering stop beside the Suwantek Systems freighter. But then an oval hatch opened and a ramp lowered to the docking bay floor. A girl stepped out. She wore a crisp, black uniform. She had black hair, blue skin, and bright red eyes.

Nuru was stunned. Stepping cautiously forward, he said, "Veeren?"

The girl looked at him quizzically. "Kung'urama'nuruodo."

Hearing her say his actual Chiss name, Nuru's mouth felt suddenly dry. "You . . . I . . . I'm sorry. I didn't expect to see you again."

"No, you did not." Without taking her eyes off him, she continued, "Your allies may reveal themselves without apprehension. I traveled alone. I am unarmed. I will not damage them."

"Of course," Nuru said, although he had a ha[rd] time imagining Veeren posing much of a threa[t] Breakout Squad. "You can come out, men. It'[s] Aristocra." He noticed Veeren wince slightly pronunciation.

The troopers and Cleaver stepped o[ut] behind the cargo containers and moved Nuru. Veeren cast a quick glance at the tr[oopers] the droid, then returned her gaze to Nuru. "Your mechanical translator located the transmitter I placed on Captain Lalo Gunn's freighter."

"What?" Nuru looked at Cleaver. "Cleaver, do you understand what she's talking about?"

"I believe so." The droid reached down and removed the magnetic cylinder from his thigh. Handing it to Nuru, he said, "I *thought* it was the transmitter. I found it on the hull. It's a good thing Captain Gunn told me to save it for later."

Returning his gaze to Veeren, Nuru said, "*You* put the transmitter on the *Harpy*?"

"I have admitted this fact."

"But . . . why?"

Veeren looked stung. "Why did I admit this?"

"No," Nuru said, feeling suddenly exasperated. "Why did you plant the transmitter?"

Veeren blinked and lifted her chin a fraction. "It enabled me to follow you across space. I see Captain Lalo Gunn is no longer traveling with you."

"No, she isn't, she . . ." Nuru struggled to find words. He realized if Cleaver had not found the transmitter, Veeren might have tracked the device to Gunn's crashed ship on Vaced. He considered telling Veeren about the crash but quickly decided it had little bearing on their current circumstances. "Veeren, may I ask why you followed us all the way from Chiss space?"

"I followed *you*, Kung'urama'nuruodo, because I am compelled to tell you something of great importance."

Nuru waited. "Yes?"

"An analysis of several events, including the Separatist attack on Chiss Expansionary Defense Force Station Ifpe'a, has determined a high probability that you are an unwitting accomplice to an unknown individual or group whose goal is galactic domination."

Nuru was taken aback. Breaker said, "I beg your pardon, Aristocra, but . . . you're suggesting someone has been using Commander Nuru? To help conquer the galaxy?"

"Actually," Veeren said, "it is quite possible we are all being manipulated."

The Sith, Nuru thought. *She must be talking about the Sith.* Before he could ask Veeren if she had any knowledge of the existence of the Sith Lords, she faced him and continued, "Although I do not have conclusive evidence, I suspect a conspiracy may date back over eleven of your standard years, when the Jedi discovered you as an infant, adrift in a Chiss escape pod in the Outer Rim. I also suspect that because you are Chiss as well as a Jedi, you are in great danger. Perhaps you should investigate."

Although Nuru thought Veeren's suspicions about a conspiracy were incredible, he said, "You should come with us to Coruscant. We can inform the Jedi Council and—"

"You will tell no one of our conversation," Veeren interrupted. "The Chiss Ascendancy is unaware of my data analysis or my suspicions. Except for you and the members of your team, no one else knows I have left Chiss space. I have taken many precautions to maintain secrecy because I believe there *is* a conspiracy, and spies and assassins could be anywhere. The conspirators will not hesitate to silence anyone who speaks of them or interferes with their plans. If you alert your Jedi Council to anything I have said, you risk my life as well as your own."

"I understand," Nuru said, even though he doubted there were spies in the Jedi Council.

"I must go." Veeren turned abruptly and began walking back to her hovering ship.

"What?" Nuru said. "Wait! Where are you going?"

Veeren stopped and glanced back at him. "I am returning to Chiss space."

"But . . . now I *don't* understand. You traveled days to track me down, just to warn me that someone might be trying to take over the galaxy, and then you leave?"

Veeren cocked her head. "It seems that you understand perfectly." And then she resumed walking toward her ship's landing ramp. Nuru suddenly realized he was still clutching the cylindrical transmitter.

Veeren entered her ship. The landing ramp retracted, and the oval hatch sealed. As her ship began gliding out of the docking bay, Nuru and Breakout Squad saw another starship approaching from the surrounding asteroid field. The incoming ship's running lights were off.

Ring-Sol Ambase and the clone trooper who claimed his name was Sharp were seated in the cockpit of the Kuat *Corona*-class transport that had just arrived at Bilbringi VII. Their journey from the Bogden system had been long, but Ambase had spent much of the time using Jedi meditation techniques to regain his strength. Still, he was not fully recovered, and because they did not know what they might encounter at Bilbringi Depot, they were being especially cautious. At Ambase's instructions, the clone had switched off the transport's running lights so they could approach the depot with some discretion.

But as they neared one of the docking bays, they sighted a bizarre teardrop-shaped vessel gliding toward them. A warning light flashed on the *Corona*'s nav console. The clone said, "We're being scanned, General, but . . . that ship it . . . it isn't appearing on our sensors!"

The mysterious vessel suddenly glowed brightly. "It's definitely not a Republic ship," Ambase said with concern. Neither he nor the clone saw the Republic troopers who were in the docking bay beyond the glowing ship.

An alarm sounded from the *Corona*'s console panel. "We're picking up massive radiation emissions," the clone said. "They may be charging weapons." The clone's hands flew to the controls for the transport's laser cannon as the glowing ship suddenly increased intensity and accelerated toward the transport.

Three laser beams streaked from the glowing ship and smashed against the *Corona*'s shields. Ambase said, "Return fire."

The Corona's cannon fired straight at the glowing ship. Ambase had assumed that the bizarre ship was heavily shielded. He was genuinely startled to see the single volley of laser fire cause the ship to explode in a brilliant burst of light.

The explosion lifted Nuru, the troopers, and Cleaver off their feet and sent them crashing across the docking bay deck. Nuru dropped the transmitter as he rolled and jumped to his feet. He snatched his lightsaber from his belt and ignited it while stray bits of glowing metal trailed away from the explosion. He gasped. "No."

The glowing wreckage illuminated the vessel that had destroyed Veeren's ship. The attacking vessel was a Kuat *Corona*-class transport. Nuru directed his gaze at the transport and shouted, "No!"

Inside the *Corona*, Ring-Sol Ambase sensed a disturbance in the Force, a wave of anger so strong that it jolted him in his seat. He shuddered with the terrible realization that the anger was directed at him and that it came from someone he knew.

Nuru?!

And then he sensed Nuru's awareness of him. A moment later, he felt an even stronger wave of rage crash over him.

Ambase suddenly feared Count Dooku had been telling the truth about Nuru turning against him. He also knew he was not sufficiently recovered to confront his Padawan.

He looked at the clone beside him and said, "Get us out of here. Now!"

The clone jerked the controls, and the transport raced away from Bilbringi Depot.

The troopers and Cleaver picked themselves up from the docking bay deck and moved toward Nuru, who was still holding his lightsaber and facing a cluster of asteroids where he had lost sight of the *Corona*. Breaker looked at Nuru and said, "Are you all right, Commander?"

Nuru stammered, "My—my Master was on the transport . . . that fired at Veeren's ship."

Cleaver said, "Your Master? General Ambase? But . . . why?"

Breaker looked at the other troopers. He knew that they, like him, had no idea how to proceed. And as they waited for Nuru's next order, none of them noticed the lone battle droid who crept out from a nearby maintenance hatch. The droid carried a blaster rifle. He aimed it at the troopers and opened fire.

"Take *that*, Republic dogs!" the droid said as he shot one trooper in the back. The trooper collapsed, his armored body clattering against the deck.

The other troopers and Cleaver spun fast and

were about to return fire when they saw Nuru was already racing straight for the droid, swinging his lightsaber back and forth to deflect the fired energy bolts away from his allies. The droid cried, "Oh, no!" Nuru's blade swept through the droid's neck and torso. The droid's parts fell to the deck.

Nuru darted back to the troopers. The droid's attack had happened so fast that Nuru had not seen which trooper had been shot, but then he heard one of the three unharmed troopers say, "Chatterbox! Can you hear me?" It was Breaker's voice.

Chatterbox groaned.

"Get his helmet off," said Breaker as he carefully rolled Chatterbox over, elevating his shoulders and head while Knuckles plucked an emergency med kit from his belt.

Sharp removed Chatterbox's helmet. Grimacing, Chatterbox gasped out, "I think it's bad."

Just then, Gizz returned to the docking bay. He was carrying a sack that he had stuffed with food rations and was chewing on a large stick of nerf jerky. Seeing the group huddled around the fallen trooper, he said, "Did I miss something?"

Ignoring Gizz, Nuru said, "Sharp and Breaker!

Sweep the area! Make sure there aren't any more battle droids!" Nuru returned his attention to helping Chatterbox.

Breaker and Sharp left the others, running past Gizz to the maintenance hatch. Breaker said, "I'll take the hatch. You search the outer corridor." Breaker entered the hatch.

Sharp proceeded to the corridor that lay beyond the docking bay. The corridor was empty. Keeping his rifle in front of him, he kept moving until he found a metal door for a storage room. He kicked the door open and jumped in, ready to shoot even a simple cleaning droid. The storage room was also empty.

Sharp glanced back into the corridor, then stepped into the room and shut the door behind him. Leaning against the door, he removed his helmet and took a series of deep breaths. And as he breathed, his facial muscles shifted. His smooth, pale skin changed to a dusky, grayish green. He squeezed his eyes shut, and when he opened them again, they were yellow and reptilian.

He thought of what might have happened to him if he had been shot and the members of Breakout

Squad had removed his helmet to see his true face. He shuddered. He knew that now was hardly the time to relax. He still had work to do.

The Clawdite shape-shifter took another deep breath, pulled on his helmet, and then made his way back to the clone troopers.

Lalo Gunn pushed her empty glass back and forth across the crackled surface of the bar in the dimly lit tavern at Vaced Spaceport. There were only a few other customers at the bar, and Gunn was ignoring all of them. The bartender, a Qiraash with high cheekbones and a much higher forehead, looked at Gunn and said, "You finished?"

"Oh, I'm finished, all right," Gunn said, shifting on her seat. The bartender took the glass. Gunn placed a credit chip on the bar. She was about to get up when a large man moved up beside her and placed a hand on the shoulder. She glared at the man. He pointed to the raised stool next to hers, and said, "This seat taken?"

"I was just leaving," Gunn said.

"Stay awhile longer," the man said, keeping one hand on her shoulder. "I've got credits. I'll buy us a round of—"

"If you want to keep your hand," a deep voice interrupted from behind Gunn, "you'll remove it from the lady and be on your way."

The man laughed. "Oh, yeah? Who's gonna make me?" Grinning broadly, he glanced back to see who was standing behind Gunn. The man's grin vanished, and he suddenly looked nervous. "I meant no harm," the man said as he yanked his hand away from Gunn and hurried out of the tavern.

"It's about time you got here," Gunn said as the newcomer sat down beside her. "When you hired me on Kynachi, I didn't bargain losing the *Harpy*. You said there'd be a big reward for me if I got Breakout Squad to Vaced. I expect to be well paid."

"You needn't worry about your reward," Cad Bane said with a smile that bared his sharp teeth.

NEXT:

Star Wars: The Clone Wars Secret Missions #4: Guardians of the Chiss Key

Devastated by the explosive events at Bilbringi Depot, Nuru Kungurama returns to the Jedi Temple on Coruscant while the remaining members of Breakout Squad await their next mission. But after an alien escape pod vanishes from the Jedi Archives, Nuru finds himself flung toward a fateful encounter with his own Jedi Master, Ring-Sol Ambase.

ABOUT THE AUTHOR

A former editor of *Star Wars* and *Indiana Jones* comics, Ryder Windham has written over sixty books, including *Star Wars: The Ultimate Visual Guide* (DK Publishing), *A New Hope: The Life of Luke Skywalker* (Scholastic), and *Indiana Jones and the Pyramid of the Sorcerer* (Harper Collins UK and Scholastic). He lives in Providence, Rhode Island, with his family.

ABOUT THE COVER ARTIST

Wayne Lo served as Art Director on the video game *Lair* as well as spent six years in Industrial Light & Magic's art department, where he cursed pirates, skinned werewolves, skewered vampires, and thawed Neverland before joining the design team for Lucasfilm's *Star Wars: The Clone Wars* animated series.